# the
# rhyming
# season

# the rhyming season

# EDWARD AVERETT

*Clarion Books*
New York

Clarion Books
a Houghton Mifflin Company imprint
215 Park Avenue South, New York, NY 10003
Text copyright © 2005 by Edward Averett

The text was set in 12-point Berkeley Book.

www.houghtonmifflinbooks.com

Printed in the U.S.A.

Library of Congress Cataloging-in-Publication Data

Averett, Edward, 1951–
The rhyming season / by Edward Averett.
p. cm.
Summary: A senior basketball player shoulders the hopes of a dying mill
town and her bereaved family when she and an eccentric English
teacher–coach try to lead their team to state basketball history.
ISBN 0-618-46948-6
[1. Grief—Fiction. 2. Brothers—Fiction. 3. Basketball—Fiction.
4. Sawmills—Fiction. 5. High schools—Fiction. 6. Schools—Fiction.
7. Coaches (Athletics)—Fiction.] I. Title.
PZ7.A9345Rhy 2005
[Fic]—dc22
2005007046

ISBN-13: 978-0-618-46948-2
ISBN-10: 0-618-46948-6

QUM 10 9 8 7 6 5 4 3 2 1

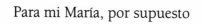

Para mi María, por supuesto

*It's little I care what path I take,*
*And where it leads it's little I care;*
*But out of this house, lest my heart break,*
*I must go, and off somewhere.*

—Edna St. Vincent Millay, "Departure"

# Chapter 1

Jen was braver than all of us, so she was the one who actually made our tree the tallest in Lewis County. I went along and carried the saw. It wasn't really like me, but I did it because the boys chickened out at the last minute and we had to do something about Napavine. You might wonder how an entire girls' basketball team could sneak into town under the noses of their biggest rivals, but we didn't have a game that night and Napavine was playing a Class A school up by Olympia. So nobody was there to actually catch us.

My town of Hemlock, Washington, is named after a tree. Not after a famous American, not after an ancient city in Europe, but after a type of evergreen tree that resides on the same part of the earth we do. We make our living from the hemlock and a few others like it, but we don't take the trees for granted, like some people do. We've worshiped them for as far back as anyone can remember. That's why we would risk life and limb to shinny up the wimpy Douglas fir that stands in front of the Napavine City Hall and lop six feet off the top so that our tree, the mighty hemlock in front of our City Hall, would be the tallest in Lewis County.

What made it especially good was that our boys' team was at a scrimmage in Evaline, so they all had alibis. And nobody would have thought to blame the girls' team for such a boy thing to do. Girls in Hemlock weren't expected to do much of anything. Maybe that's why it made our team even stronger. It helped us jell as a unit, and I think it made us believe we could win it all. Our coach, Ms. Cochran, had told us we were headed for big things. She said that when a team gets as close as we had the year before and takes risks the way we had, it can only spell future success on the court. We believed her and took every opportunity to let it be known.

In fact, people might have gotten sick of us marching down Main/56, weaving in and out of our line. Jen, Freddie, Mavis, Lena, and I clapped and sang with every bounce. Some of the players from the boys' team would yell at us from their cars, and it only made us bolder. It made us raise our voices so we were practically screaming through town. Mom said we sounded like an army drill regiment as we sang, "Go Jacks, go Jacks, go Jacks," till our voices cracked like raspy old saws. Jen always brought us back on key. She was the team leader; we all focused on which way she was going to move. Being 6'1", I kind of stuck out in the middle of the pack, but that didn't keep us from being smooth. We meshed together like we were all one body. We might as well have been. We'd been born and raised in Hemlock. Tree sap was the glue that held us together.

After the cutting we took our turns guarding the new tallest tree in Lewis County, to protect it from anyone who had a plan to make it shorter. We all smirked at one another. It was fun being the only ones who knew we had made it happen. When our shift was done, the boys' team would take over for us. We'd slap their hands like it was a tag-team wrestling match. Some of the boys suspected what we'd done, and I think they actually appreciated it. I know my brother, Benny, did. Not enough to give the girls any credit for it, though. Those were the good old days in Hemlock: things moved like they were supposed to. But that was last year. Things are a little different now.

I come from a family of tall people. In my town that makes you better at trimming the high spots on trees or playing basketball. Sometimes both. My dad, Buzzy Jacobsen, is one of those. He was a foreman at the Fostoria Mill and also known as the best damn basketball player ever to come out of the area. He's 6'3" and the kind of guy who bowls you over. My mom, Merilee Jacobsen, is 5'11", but Grandpa Jacobsen always said the tape measure was off and she's taller than that. Grandpa used to run the town barbershop, and I guess it was his job to size up the new prospects.

We reached our peak in 1981, my dad's senior year, when the boys' team went to the state tournament. But after that basketball's future in Hemlock was looking grim. Mom says you could see all the boys in town lined up outside the barbershop, and not a one of them broke six feet. So when my mom and dad went on their first date the year after graduation, visions of a state championship just a generation away dazzled all the men in town. Grandpa gave them money to go out, and all the parents turned their heads the other way when Mom and Dad drove to the parking lot of the Fostoria Mill to get to know each other better. All that for the future of basketball. And people say arranged marriages happen only in other cultures.

I live in a desperate town. Just outside the town limits is a sign that Grandpa Jacobsen bought and paid for. It says:

*Welcome to Hemlock*
*Home of the 1981 Boys' Class B Basketball*
*Ninth Place Finisher*

Lots of small towns have these signs, but here's the thing: There is no ninth place in Washington State high school basketball. My town made it up. There are only eight places. Sure they went to State, and they almost got a trophy, but they were eliminated on the next-to-last day and finished just out of the running. So there you have it. In my town all your hopes and dreams boil down to two things: hoops and trees.

Grandpa Jacobsen's plan to produce a star player actually almost worked. On their first try Mom and Dad came up with a baby boy, my brother, Benny, who was the smoothest, smartest, most confident player since my dad. In his junior year Benny broke my dad's league records for scoring and rebounding. He led the Hemlock Lumberjacks to the brink of the state tournament, losing to Adna on a controversial call at the buzzer that the people of Hemlock still write letters to the editor about. That ref will never work the Western Lewis County League again.

Hemlock was all set for Benny's senior year. This was going to be it—the year of years. Finally, all that hard work was going to pay off. My parents had already reserved a room for five nights in March at the Davenport Hotel in Spokane, where the Class B tournament is held every year. We were good sports and braved a so-so football season. Then we rejoiced when basketball practice officially started in November. It was my junior year, and I was taking it all in. I was on the girls' team, and we were no slouches ourselves. Under the expert coaching of Ms. Cochran, and with a little help from her assistant, Mr. Hobbs, we ended up winning eighteen out of twenty-six games that season, and I was the leading scorer.

The boys and girls practiced at opposite ends of the gym, and sometimes I stopped what I was doing just to watch my brother. It reminded me of a slow-motion shot of a racehorse, the way its muscles flex and stretch and gather together in a bunch as it runs. He galloped around the court like a thoroughbred. The first game of the season he scored thirty-two points, but he didn't strut around pounding his chest like some guys would. He took it calmly and hit the practice court the following day, preparing for the next game. Benny was a pro.

That season the Lumberjacks won their first six games, including a big home win over Napavine. Benny was averaging twenty-eight points a game. The team was winning by big margins. The whole town was one big happy family. The first polls came out, and we were ranked seventh in the state. My dad and all his friends at the Jacobsen Barber Emporium were grabbing the boys off the street and putting them up against the doorjamb of the shop, checking to see if they'd grown any in the past few days. That doorjamb is filled with pencil marks and initials from clear back to the Stone Age. It was shaping up to be a guaranteed dream season. Then right after the New Year came the night of the Boistfort game.

The bleachers were packed, and everyone was screaming. People actually had to stand three deep by the stage next to the court in order to watch the game. It sure made the fire marshal nervous. That night we girls won our game by fifteen, and afterward the boys took theirs by an even twenty. My mom was hugging my dad, and a college scout stopped to talk to my parents for a few minutes after the game. It was a big night in Hemlock. But you can have all the fun and laughter and hope and promise in one second, and in the next second all those things can take wing and fly to someone else's town.

After the Boistfort game, Benny and his friends drove around the back roads celebrating the big win. Sometime in the middle of the night Benny said goodbye to them and started to drive home. What happened next would have made sense if Benny had been drinking, but there wasn't a drop of alcohol in his veins. So it's still a mystery why his car left the road at ninety miles an hour and slammed into one of those very same evergreen trees that our town is named after.

The wreck was discovered just a half hour later, but by then my brother's life was over. And that's when things started to change. For me and for everybody in Hemlock.

Chapter 2

Hemlock is like any other lumber town you'll come across. It's surrounded by trees, and a permanent layer of smoke hovers over the whole scene. Practically everyone works at the mill. And then there're the endless sounds of trees meeting their ends. Day after day we hear the whir of the saws, the splash of the logs falling into the slough, the grind of the planer mill as it shaves the bark, the rattle of sawdust chips as they travel up the narrow pipes and are spit out onto the big blond pile. All 737 of us live with that racket every day, so it's no wonder you often think about the trees that make it all happen.

The summer before my senior year, I found myself thinking about the trees more than usual. It was part of my A.B. life. After Benny. It was a drifting life, not in the sense of what I did, but in the way my mind worked. I have a theory that when life is going well, all those electrical connections in the brain fire like they've had a tune-up. When bad things happen, you get a short up there and just drift, waiting for the time when the sparks come around again.

On those days I liked to walk down to City Hall and climb the tallest tree in Lewis County. Once I was up there, I could see that Hemlock is surrounded by hills. Hairy hills. At least it looked that way from far up. The town is about five miles from the interstate, and one of the things these hills do is shield us from any freeway noise that might filter into town late at night. It makes me feel like all of us are out in the middle of nowhere, far away from the rest of the world.

In some places the hills are still jam-packed with prickly evergreen trees. But in the last few years some of the hills have started getting haircuts. On the west end of town you can see a bald hill with a dark evergreen Mohawk down the middle. Selective logging, they call it. The hill on the south side is more of a grass green. That comes from the clearcutting they did about twenty years ago, when they cleaned out all the trees and planted new ones. They come up a lighter green when they're young. With the trees thinning out so fast, we should have known what was going to happen next.

My dad, his dad, and his dad before him worked at the mill. It's a way of life, an expectation. Whenever a baby boy is born in Hemlock, people will say two things about him: "He'll make a good shooting guard" and "He's got a millwright's hands."

So you can imagine the big deal it made only eight months after Benny died when the whole town went quiet in the middle of the night. Even I heard it. After a lifetime of mill noise, silence has a voice, and it woke me up. Something was wrong, but I didn't quite know what it was. I heard our front door open, so I went down to check it out.

I found my dad standing in our front yard in his underwear. Our next-door neighbor, Darwin Ostrander—from the '80 team that got lost in the snowstorm before the Winlock game—was doing the same. In fact, all down the block guys were standing outside in their underwear, checking their watches and sniffing the air like something was cooking. My mom and I stayed on the front steps. She put her arm around me.

"What is it?" I asked her.

"It's not good" was all she said.

Then my dad started swearing. Not the generic run-of-the-mill kind you can hear on satellite TV, but really decent original stuff. My dad can be very creative. But when it got down to what he was really mad about, he just threw his head back and howled like a wolf. "Jolley!"

Mr. Jolley is the superintendent of the Fostoria Mill. He has a son, Eric, who's tall enough for me to date but who has two left feet on the court. He's smart and has model looks, though, which has only seemed to add to the fact that a lot of people see his family as kind of snobbish. They've had more money than anybody else in Hemlock since the town began.

After he yelled, Dad took off running for his old International pickup. This got my mom's attention.

"Buzzy!" she called. "What are you doing?"

But Dad started up his truck without ever answering. Gravel flew every which way when he backed out and sped off down the street.

"Oh, Lord, Brenda," my mom said. "Get something on and come with me."

Mom and I took off in her Monte Carlo, and it looked like most of the town was following us to the mill. When we got to the parking lot, I saw the International parked sideways, with the engine still running and the driver's door hanging open.

A good crowd was already at the main door when we got there. And I could see why. My dad had Lester Jolley on the floor and was straddling him. Vern Castleman, a guy from the '76 team, who was kicked out at District for having sex in the concession stand at the Olequa gym, was standing near us. "What's going on?" my mom asked him.

Vern shrugged. "Fostoria closed down the mill."

"For the night?" she asked.

"Looks like for good," he said.

Sometimes when you've had a big loss in your life, you think there's no more room for shock or tears. But that night at the mill I felt my stomach do flip-flops again. We were saying goodbye to a way of life.

Mr. Jolley started shouting at my dad. "Buzzy, they gave me the order to shut down the place. It came from Seattle. There was nothing I could do."

For a second I thought Dad had come back to his senses, but that wasn't quite the case. "There's always something that can be done, Lester," he growled. "You're just too chicken to not do what they say."

"Let me go," Mr. Jolley pleaded. "It affects all of us, Buzzy. Not just you."

My mom sucked in her breath. Everybody did. I looked away, not wanting to see what was coming next. And instead I found myself looking at Eric Jolley standing just on the edge of a circle of light by the door. His eyes caught mine and held them for a second. Strange. It was as if his face showed exactly what I was feeling: We both were expecting the worst of our dads.

But my dad caught my attention again, because instead of starting a big brawl, he uncurled his fist and crawled off Mr. Jolley. Mr. Jolley got up and dusted himself off. Relief filled the room. My mom reached down and squeezed my hand. She yelled over to my dad, "It's going to be all right, Buzzy."

And I honestly thought it was going to be. Until Mr. Jolley continued.

"Yeah, Buzzy," said Mr. Jolley. "Besides, I think we all know this isn't really about the mill."

Something bad had built a home in my dad since Benny had left us. He used to be someone I looked up to. When he and Benny called me into the family room to watch a game with them, I'd come running. Or out in the driveway, he used to stop and take the basketball from my hands. "You need to hold it like this, Bren," he'd say, and so I would. At night he used to come up the stairs and tell Benny it was lights out, and then he'd stop by my room and stick his head in. "You too, kid. Can't let the early birds get the best of you." Back then he made you want to be better in everything you did. But not now. Not this dad.

This dad leaned down and picked up a thick piece of lumber and waved it high above his head.

"I hate this damn town!" he roared, and he started swinging. The crowd took a few steps back but stayed to watch my dad take out his vengeance on the mill. He slammed compressors, broke light bulbs, and kicked in panels.

Vern started clapping, slowly at first and then like one of those Spanish flamenco dancers. The rest of the crowd did the same.

"You show them, Buzz," Darwin said. There was a quaver in

his voice that'd been there ever since he spent some time at the state mental hospital.

Then the Schultz twins joined in. They're not identical, except in their stupidity. "They can't do this to us," Stan said. You could tell he and his brother, Stew, had been out drinking. They both clapped out of rhythm.

I couldn't stay and watch anymore. I slipped my hand from my mom's and took off for the car. On the way, I stopped at the International and turned off the ignition. When I closed the door, I saw Eric Jolley walking to his car, which was parked a few down from ours.

"Can't take it either, huh?" he said.

"No," I said. I could still hear the clapping and the shouts coming from inside.

Eric walked over to me. "I guess he's not too happy about the mill closing."

"My dad? No, I don't think he is."

"Mine, neither," he said. "Only he was the one on the bottom."

"Sorry about that. My dad—well, you know my dad."

"I don't think mine is much different. He always takes it about one sentence too far." He leaned against the front fender and crossed his arms. "I can't wait to get out of here," he said.

I looked over to the mill. "It may go on for a while."

"No, I mean out of here. Out of Hemlock."

"You're leaving?"

"Sure. Aren't you? I mean, graduating and going to college."

I was glad for the darkness, because I could feel my face flush. Of course he was talking about next year. "Yes. I guess so." To be honest, I really hadn't been giving it much thought.

I was having too much trouble getting through this year to worry about the next. I could have said that to him, but my mouth suddenly seemed unable to form real words. "You know, a lot's been going on in my life." I'd known Eric since kindergarten, maybe even before that. So I shouldn't have been feeling that nervous talking to a guy I saw every day of the year.

"Hear that?" he said. Above the clapping came the faint sound of a siren. "I think my old man just called for reinforcements. I'm going to get out of here. You okay?"

"Yes. Yes I am." I shuffled my feet. "I have to find my mom."

"Sure thing. Well, see you around."

I watched him walk over to his car. A bright, shiny, new Honda. The benefits of having money, I guess.

I hurried over to the Monte Carlo, where my mom was already waiting for me. "Who was that?" she asked.

"Eric Jolley," I said.

"Don't get anything started with him, Brenda."

"Mom!" I didn't know if I was more embarrassed or surprised she would even think about that. Not that every girl in my class hadn't thought about the possibility. But it seemed like there had always been an unspoken agreement between Eric and me because of our fathers. There were no bad feelings, but we gave each other space. Maybe we were trying to end the long history of animosity between our two families. When Benny died, Eric was the only boy who came up to me after the funeral and told me he was sorry. But other than that, the few minutes I'd spoken to him tonight was the longest conversation we'd ever had.

Mom sighed like somebody had just put the whole world

directly on her shoulders. "We'd better go, honey," she said. "We'll deal with your father later."

As we drove home, I thought about my dad. I knew it was hard for him. That's what Mom had been saying all spring and summer. That's why he stayed out so late. That's why he drove around the back roads until he ran out of gas. That's why he took a basketball and played by himself out on the elementary school playground court. And now this. My dad had never been afraid to speak what was on his mind. But now he seemed to have only bad things to say. And his voice was louder and meaner sometimes.

I knew exactly what he was going through, because I was feeling it too. I just kept it all inside. My stomach rumbled with my own fears and complaints. That night my dad ended up in the municipal jail, but I didn't need those artificial bars. I carried my cage along with me.

Highway 56 becomes Main Street for the half mile it cuts through the middle of town. If you stand at one end of Main/56 and look straight ahead, you can pretty much see the whole town. The last sign you can see is for Maida's Drugstore. Next to that is the Fir Cone, and across the street is the Pine Cone. These are taverns, and lately they've been getting the most business in town, especially from the Schultz twins. Then there's Marv's Videos, the Hemlock Thrift Store, and the Palm Café. Next to the café is an empty lot where Myklebust's clothing store used to be before the fire that the '73 team put out single-handedly—but not before the building was a total loss. Next to the lot is the City Hall. It sits back from Main/56 and has our famous tree out front. The police station is next door. Then come the schools all bunched together. The elementary school is next to the middle school, which is connected to Hemlock High. Most everybody I know walked into kindergarten on one end of the building and, twelve years later, walked out the other end with a diploma.

Across the street from the police station are two vacant buildings, then the Cut 'n' Curl, and then the Jacobsen Barber Emporium. My dad isn't actually a barber, but he inherited the shop after Grandpa died. Once in a while some guy will actually get a haircut there, but mostly my dad and his friends just use it as a place to gather and talk basketball.

The jail is behind the police station, and I was standing across the street when they let my dad out the next day. He had been charged with malicious mischief, which means he ended up doing some real damage to the mill. Mom pulled up, and my dad slunk into her car. When they drove away, I saw Jen and Freddie crossing the street.

Jen was wearing jeans and a T-shirt that said GET OVER YOURSELF. I don't like to wear clothing that people can read. My mom says that's why Jen and I are so close: Opposites attract, is her philosophy. Jen walked over, pulling her hair back into a ponytail. "Looks like your dad was a bad boy," she said.

"Leave her alone," said Freddie. Freddie is sometimes a little too bossy, but I like it when she puts Jen in her place and I don't have to.

"Where's Mavis?" I asked.

"We were helping her and her mom paint the laundry room," Freddie said. "Mavis and Lena stayed to finish. Thanks to your friend here, there's more paint on them than on the walls."

Jen grinned and shrugged her shoulders. "It was an accident," she said.

I noticed Freddie had some paint splotches on her shoes. Her jeans looked a little ragged too, but she didn't pay much attention to that sort of thing. She was the prettiest of all of us, but she hated being told that. "Sorry about your dad," she said.

"That's okay." My friends had known my family and me forever. They had seen my dad at his best and, now, at his worst. They'd been through it all with me.

We walked across the street and sat on the bench in front of the police station. We watched cars go by for a while. Most of them I recognized, but a couple were from out of town. One was from Montana, and I started to wonder what it would be like there. Not knowing anyone and no one knowing me: who I was, who I used to be, or what had happened with Benny.

Jen noticed I was quiet. "What's up with you?" she asked. "You look like you just saw a ghost."

I saw the look that passed between Freddie and Jen. I knew that later Freddie would call Jen and ask why she had to bring up the whole ghost thing since I'd lost my brother. I hated it when people were careful around me.

"It's nothing," I said.

Freddie started working hard to come up with something to talk about. "So you think it'll be Lena playing forward this year?" she asked.

"That's up to Ms. Cochran," said Jen.

"Then she needs to work on her jump shot," said Freddie.

"What she needs to do is grow about three inches," Jen said.

I looked up then to see Eric Jolley driving by in his Honda. He slowed for the speed bump and smiled at me as he drove over it. I thought about my talk with him in the dark the night before and smiled back.

"What was that about?" asked Jen.

"What?" I asked innocently.

"I didn't know you were friends with Eric Jolley."

"I'm not. But it's not like we're enemies, either," I told her.

"Whatever you say."

The three of us watched his car until it was out of sight. Then Jen looked over at me. "He's gone now," she said. "So you can probably stop smiling."

I hadn't realized I still was. But I stopped it real quick once I did.

I watched a TV show once where high school students were shocked to know that their teachers had actual lives outside of school. They should have been living in Hemlock. Some of the teachers did live way out of town or in another town altogether, but most were our neighbors. Ms. Cochran lived only a block from Lena's house, which is only two blocks from Mavis's. People say you have to be on your best behavior if you're a teacher living in the town you work in. It's hard to be a good role model if your students can see you being hauled off by Officer Parsons after a bad Saturday night.

But Ms. Cochran never had that problem. The health class we had with her was the best class I ever took, but that's not why we liked her. She seemed more like a friend. She knew the right thing to do all the time. She'd be in your face when you deserved it, but she'd also leave you alone when you needed it. The girls on the team had developed a habit of showing up at her place at odd hours because she made the mistake of telling us we were always welcome. She'd never let on whether that was a problem or not.

She was home when we knocked, and she let us right in. She asked right away about Mavis and Lena, and we explained their absence.

"It's a well-known fact," she said, "that helping out with the family is the only acceptable thing that can interfere with the team." Ms. Cochran was big on team with a capital T.

Her house was like a tidy locker room. The small living room was filled with gym bags, a treadmill, a stationary bike, and a table covered with perfectly stacked school papers. It looked like she was planning for the new year.

She brought in some bottles of Gatorade, and we all sat on the couch after she pulled off a pile of folded laundry.

"Okay," she said. "First things first. This isn't a practice, right?"

"Right," Jen, Freddie, and I said in unison.

"And it's not a team meeting."

"Definitely not," said Jen. The state has rules about teams getting together before the formal date when practice season begins.

"Okay, then. What's up?"

"We think Four-point should start this year," Jen said.

Ms. Cochran furrowed her brow. "Who's Four-point?"

"You know. Lena," Jen said. We called Lena that because of her GPA.

"She's really improved," I said. "You saw how she was during the summer."

"Yes, I did, and I agree. But I don't think we should be talking about other players when they're not present." And then

Ms. Cochran did something that was completely out of character for her. When she's talking, she usually stares right into your eyes. Sometimes for so long that you have to look away. But after she said that last part, her eyes looked over to the wall and stayed there. And her expression changed, as if something bad was about to happen.

"We know it's up to you," I continued. "But we worked so well together this summer. And Angie is just a junior, and we were thinking it would be cool to have all seniors start this year."

"All seniors," Freddie repeated.

"Listen. Girls," Ms. Cochran said. She licked her lips nervously, then took a sip of Gatorade.

We sat there for what seemed like minutes while Ms. Cochran finished her drink. I played with the label on mine. Jen yawned and leaned back on the couch. Freddie was trying to look over at the stuff on the table.

Finally, Ms. Cochran set her bottle down. "A lot is happening now," she said. "The mill closing is going to bring changes. We need to focus. Concentration will be the word of the year. You can't lose that, girls, no matter what happens. You have to promise me that."

"Focus is not a problem," Jen said.

"Well, then, we'll have to see what happens. We'll do everything we can to make it a great season. And that means the best starters will start."

As we were walking off Ms. Cochran's porch, Jen turned to me. "Okay, what's the deal? Did you hear her in there? Where's the real Ms. Cochran? That woman is like her evil twin."

"You noticed it too, huh?" I said. "Something's wrong."

"What do you think, Snoop?" Jen asked Freddie. Freddie has a reputation for getting into other people's business. "You see anything?"

"Just the usual stuff. Schoolwork. Bills. And that letter from Oregon."

"Letter?" Sometimes I had no patience with Freddie.

"Yep."

I think she does it on purpose. I saw Jen clench her jaw. She and Freddie have gotten into it before over this, so I stepped between the two of them.

"You saw a letter, Fred?"

She nodded. "From Oregon."

"And it wasn't a bill or an ad for a new weight set or anything?"

"Don't think so. It had an Indian name on the return. And it was from a college."

"She's always getting things from schools," Jen said. "It's probably just somebody needing a reference letter or something."

"Maybe," Freddie said. "But if you put two and two together, she's been acting different. You see her at the Burgermaster and she's all nice, but she doesn't stay and talk like she used to."

"She's totally there where basketball is concerned," Jen said. "Year round. Did you ever get a call at night so she can tell you an idea she had for a new play?"

"Maybe she got some bad news," I said. "That could be it."

"Nah," Jen said. "It's more than that. Hey, maybe she's in love or something."

But none of this felt like love to me. I stopped paying attention to the two of them as we walked over to Mavis's. Their voices faded into the background, but I could still hear Ms. Cochran's voice in my head: "The mill closing is going to bring changes." I didn't like the sound of that.

By the time we reached Mavis's house, Jen and Freddie had decided it was the mill closing that had gotten Ms. Cochran down. That cheered them up.

Mavis was on the front porch with a paintbrush in her hand and a big slash of paint on her cheek. "Thank God," she said. "Real people are here."

"Where's Lena?" Jen asked.

Mavis touched her cheek. "We had a little paint fight," she said. "She went home." I didn't blame Lena. Mavis plays forward and she's a sweetheart, but she hasn't really grown into herself yet. She talks a lot with her hands, and we have to remind her not to accidentally hurt people when she's swinging those arms around.

Jen and Freddie started toward the porch, but I hung back in the street.

"You okay?" Jen asked, turning around.

"I think I'll go home," I said.

Jen gave me a look, but she didn't question it. They went inside, and I walked down the street. Things were changing, and it didn't feel like I was ready. I still wanted life to go back to the way it was. I didn't want thoughts about Montana to be creeping in. I didn't want Ms. Cochran to act like she had a big secret. And I sure didn't want my friends to have to watch what they said around me.

I hurried home, but my feet were moving even faster than my thoughts and I nearly fell. I almost wished I had. Then I would have had a real excuse to be crying the way I was.

# Chapter 3

By the next day I was ready for school to start, but we had another week to wait. Mom and Dad had been fighting the night before, and there had been no escaping them. They used to fight once in a while, but it was worse since Benny died. Before, Benny and I would listen from upstairs, sometimes taking bets on how long it would last. But now I was upstairs alone, and the things they said to each other filtered up and felt like fingers around my neck.

I tried to drown it out by thinking about my classes for this year. Unlike Jen, I liked school and I was pretty good at it. I could solve some tough math problems, and chemistry came pretty easily too. I wasn't as good at English, even though my teacher, Mr. Hobbs, always said I had "great potential." Mr. Hobbs had been teaching for what seemed like forever, and he was a little odd. When we studied English poets, he'd wear a hat that made him look like Sherlock Holmes, or he'd speak in a really bad English accent. He was also our assistant coach for basketball, so that didn't hurt my grade.

But school was just what passed the day until it was time for my real love: basketball. It was in my blood. If I stayed away from it for too long, it felt like I had low blood sugar. So when I started feeling down after talking to Ms. Cochran and listening to my parents fight, I decided that my problem was staying away from the court too long.

The elementary school playground has a concrete court with cracks in it. In a different town grass and weeds might have time to grow up in those cracks, but here in Hemlock the court gets so much use, the weeds don't stand a chance. It was like being with an old friend out there. I started by tossing the ball up to one of the metal hoops, which had lost its chain net a long time ago. I liked to hear the clang off the backboard. After a few minutes that clang focused me.

Benny and I used to play games with shooting. We'd each ask a question and then throw the ball up. If it went through the hoop, the answer was yes. If not, it meant no.

"Is it okay to bring up Benny when I talk to my mom and dad?" I asked now. The ball bounced off the rim. "But why?" I wanted to ask. Only that wouldn't have given me a yes-or-no answer.

"Do my parents have to say mean things to each other?" This time it was a swisher.

"Are my parents going to stay together?" Of course I tried to aim perfectly on that one, but it bounced off the rim again. I had a solution for that, though. If I didn't get the right answer, I ran up to the basket, caught the ball before it hit the ground, and laid it up. I knew it was cheating, but it made me feel better.

It was always good to be alone and concentrating, because that was when I felt Benny with me. If I couldn't have him out there for real once in a while, it was a good substitute at least. He might have been able to answer some of the harder questions.

He used to stand with me at the foul line, holding my arm and teaching me to follow through. "Just do it until you get in the zone," he'd say. "Pretend shooting is like breathing. You don't need to be aware of it to do it. Close your eyes and just shoot the ball up. Over and over again till it's burned into your nerve endings." It helped, and now I'm a great foul shooter. I made nine in a row there on the playground.

I'd wanted him to do the same for my jump shot, but he didn't stick around long enough to give me that lesson. So now I had lessons with Benny even though he wasn't here anymore. They say that energy survives when a person dies. He still ran with me out on the playground. He glided at my side, lifted me up. He supported my wrist, and the shot went in. That day I worked up a sweat with my brother on the playground. For a while, at least, I was in the zone.

On the first of September, just a few days before the start of my senior year, Ms. Cochran called us together for a party. There's no law against having a party that all of us happen to show up at.

But when we got there, she wasn't acting very happy. That look I'd seen when we'd visited a few days earlier was back on her face, and it made me nervous.

"I've got some bad news, girls," she said. She paced in front of us, just like she does on the sidelines during games. I thought maybe she was going to tell us somebody couldn't play this year, but I could see that everybody was there.

She stopped pacing and shook her head. "As much as I want to lead you girls to the state championship this year, I can't pass up the opportunity that's been placed right in front of me." She paused and then said, "I've gotten a job offer at a community college down in Oregon. They want me to coach women's basketball."

It was one of those moments when you don't quite know what to say. Because we'd known her for so long and she'd taught us so much, we wanted to be happy for her. But the truth is we weren't.

Jen ended up asking the big question. "But who's going to be our coach?"

"The school board promised they'd find a replacement as soon as possible."

"But who?" Jen asked again.

"I don't know yet, Jennifer. I just heard yesterday from the college. It's all still new."

"So you're going to abandon us?" I don't know exactly where it came from, but I asked that question. It made Ms. Cochran's face crumple, and I was immediately sorry.

"Please don't think that, girls. It's the last thing I want you to think. It just happens sometimes. My high school coach left in the middle of the season, and we ended up going to the playoffs. Besides, I've known for a long time that your success on the court has a lot more to do with you girls than with me."

It was small consolation. The news had us confused. After we left Ms. Cochran's house, we all just hung around on the street, like lost ducklings wondering where their mother went.

"We were going to be so good this year," Jen said. "Now what?"

"You heard what she said," Freddie said. "It's still us."

"Yeah, but we need a coach. Who do you think keeps you from fouling out in the first three minutes of the game?" Freddie was proud of her reputation and smiled big at that one.

"What's the solution, Four-point?" Jen asked Lena. We all turned to her. Lena was the short one on the court but the smart one in school. Both Jen and Freddie had tried for years to get her to give them the answers during big tests, but Lena always held out.

"We shouldn't push it," Lena said. "What will happen will happen."

Freddie rolled her eyes. "A new coach might not let you start," she tried.

Lena frowned. "In that case, maybe we should try to figure something out."

I kept quiet, but a rush of thoughts was taking over my mind. They were all jumbling together and didn't make any sense. It seemed like everything was changing. First my brother, then the mill, now my coach. Is one person supposed to go through so much all at once? I was beginning to wonder what it was I had done to anger the gods.

But this was just the beginning. Finding out who was going to be Ms. Cochran's replacement proved to be the biggest shock of all.

# Chapter 4

School finally started, and it felt good to be a senior. Jen, Freddie, Mavis, Lena, and I hooked arms in the main hallway and dared anyone to break through as we marched along. Of course, everybody tried to, but we were pretty tight. Finally, one of the boys came up from behind and started tickling Lena, which made us all fall apart laughing.

The mill was still cold and quiet. The mill workers cleared the used clothes and books out of the Hemlock Thrift Store and held a meeting. I already had homework, but Jen and I showed up anyway. It was the first time the town had gotten together since the mill had closed.

Mr. Jolley was trying to keep everybody calm, and it worked for a while. But when Stew Schultz stood up, it was like watching a first grader on the playground.

"You know darn well Fostoria can't survive without our mill," he said. It would have seemed reasonable if he hadn't burped right at the end of the sentence.

His brother, Stan, chimed in. "I give them two weeks. Then they'll come crawling back to us."

A well-dressed woman from the county was there. She sat patiently and waited for things to calm down before walking up to the podium. She spread out some papers and looked at us like a preacher speaking to her congregation.

"It's happening all over," she said. "People are losing their jobs when mills shut down. But there's hope. The government has a program. If you've lost your job in the timber industry, you can get retrained, and the government will pay for it."

It was silent for a moment, and the air was filled with electricity, like when a storm is about to break. And it did. People suddenly jumped up and started yelling as if we were all going to be executed the next day. Mr. Jolley raised his hands and tried to calm everybody down, but nobody was listening.

Jen was laughing at the chaos, but I wasn't finding it funny. I noticed Darwin Ostrander looked pretty serious too. He was sitting off to the side, and next to him was an empty chair. Ever since his wife, Margie, died, he always sat next to an empty chair. By reflex I looked at the chair next to me. That one was empty too.

My dad stood up, and it quickly got quiet in the room. "I don't know what this government stuff means," he said. "But I think the Schultzes are right. This mill was here before we all were born. And I'm guessing it'll be here when we're all dead. What can we do without it? I'm thinking we have our unemployment for about five months. They have to open up by then, don't they?" Then he looked right at the lady from the county. "You think any of these yahoos can be retrained to do anything else? Hell, Stan here can barely spell his name, and unless there's a big opening in some shop where they want a bad speller, he's going to be out of luck."

"Now, Buzz," Mr. Jolley said, but I could see he was being careful.

"What do you want to say, Jolley?" my dad asked.

Mr. Jolley shook his head. "I think that's it."

"Then let's quit wasting our time. I for one am taking bets on when the mill opens. Anyone want to get in on it?"

That was it. My dad had spoken and said the right things. I watched the woman from the county pack up her briefcase and leave. Hemlock had decided: We would wait. They needed us and our knowledge of trees. Our strong shoulders. Our tradition. I looked at Jen, but she just shrugged.

"Go Jacks," she said.


With the whole town in shock about the mill, things were moving slower than usual in Hemlock. And I guess girls' basketball wasn't high on the agenda, because the school board was taking its time finding us a new coach. A couple of prospects were interviewed, but we weren't allowed to meet with them. People were starting to talk about the upcoming season, but the talk was mostly about the boys. Instead of worrying, I decided it would be better to focus on school for a while.

I had Mr. Hobbs for senior English. He was an excellent teacher, but sometimes it was hard to get past the way he looked. He was a short, round kind of guy, and he had sideburns that were bushy and way too long. He was the kind of person who sometimes forgot to zip up his pants—not that he ever noticed. He just lived in a world all his own. I wonder if that's not so bad. Maybe the things in this world don't bother you as much then.

On the first day of class he'd worn his own graduation gown. "Just a reminder," he'd said, "of what's in store for you at the end of the year."

He was always poking at kids to get their college applications in or pushing us in other ways. When he passed you in the hall, he would ask questions like "Quick, Brenda, who wrote 'Ode on a Grecian Urn'?" Some days it was funny, but others, I just wanted to strangle the guy.

Because he had been Ms. Cochran's assistant since I'd started high school, one thing he was always willing to talk about was basketball. He was a big fan of the game. If I was feeling down one day, all I had to do was raise my hand and ask, "Mr. Hobbs? How many steals did I get in the home game with Morton last year?"

He would stop right in the middle of his boring lecture on Charles Dickens and run to his desk drawer to pull out his big notebook stuffed with statistics. He didn't even notice the kids snickering while he searched for the answer.

"Aha!" he'd cry. Then he'd push his glasses up on his nose and say, "Six. What a game that was. We really learned how to double-team in that one. And speaking of double-teaming, what do you all think of the possibility that Tolstoy's wife actually wrote the manuscript for *War and Peace*?"

A few days after the town meeting, Mr. Hobbs was up to his old tricks. The clock was moving slowly in his class and my eyelids were feeling heavy. But I could still hear him.

"What do you think it would be like," he said, "if the old writers were living in modern times? I wonder what they would be thinking about the world today. I wonder what they would write about. Any ideas?"

As a group the class turned and glanced at the clock.

"Miss Jacobsen?" Mr. Hobbs asked. "Any ideas?"

"I don't think they would like it," I said.

"Because . . . ?"

"I don't know," I tried. "I mean, I barely like it and I've been here for a while."

Luckily, the bell rang then. But unfortunately, Mr. Hobbs had this nasty habit of running over to the door and saying goodbye to us on our way out.

"Toodles," he said. "Until we meet again." He grabbed my arm and swung me out of line. "Miss Jacobsen, are we all right today?"

"Yeah, sure," I said. "Just a little tired."

"Well, perk up. Things will get better. And I think the school board will have an answer about your new coach before you know it. In fact, I believe it will be announced before the fortnight is over."

"The fortnight, Mr. Hobbs?"

"Read your assignment, Miss Jacobsen. Understanding requires an application to the process of learning."

Mr. Hobbs was right, and I started getting excited about the announcement of our new coach. It even helped me at home, where Mom and Dad were in a truce stage, which meant they were barely speaking to each other. Dinner was the worst. Before Benny died, I was hardly able to get a word in. Everyone was talking about Benny's current basketball season or the upcoming season or the one that had just passed. If I tried to say anything else, like "I got an A in math," the three of them would stop and stare at me as if they'd forgotten I was there. Then they'd congratulate me before starting up again. It was Benny this and Benny that. I didn't complain, because it was fun and I loved talking about Benny as much as they did. Now dinner was as uncomfortable as eating at someone else's house. It seemed like we were all waiting for Benny to tell us about his day.

Sometimes Mom and I tried to get a conversation going.

"How is school going?" she asked that night.

"Good," I said. "Mr. Hobbs is making us read *Pride and Prejudice*."

"What is this?" my dad interrupted. He was poking at his macaroni and cheese.

"You know what it is," Mom said.

She looked across at me and bit at her lip.

"It's good," I tried.

"If you say so," Dad growled.

And that was the end of the discussion. No fun and games. No Benny kicking me under the table. No Dad so excited about basketball he was almost yelling. No Mom rolling her eyes and eating everything on her plate. My stomach hurt, and I struggled between excusing myself and staying and taking it. I didn't really want to leave them. It felt like I was the only thing keeping us together as a family.

After dinner Dad grabbed a basketball from the closet and headed outside. Through the kitchen window I watched him dribbling down the street.

"Where's he going now?" Mom asked.

"I'll go check," I said.

I caught up with him at the elementary school court. I stood by the lilac hedge on the other side of the playground so he couldn't see me. The air was cool and misty, like it always is in the fall.

The court was empty. When he bounced the ball, the sound echoed clear over to the wall of the school. The first shot he put up went right through. In better days the sound of the ball going through the hoop would have rung through the town. Pretty soon guys from all over would have walked or driven to the playground to see what was going on.

I've spent all my life watching my dad play basketball. Watching guys play in general, for that matter. Girls' basketball hasn't been around that long, and the girls' teams haven't done very well. The boys have a long tradition, and it's hard to change tradition when a whole town is behind it. That's why the boys could assume that the court was theirs. Jen hates it, and she tries to stand up to the younger ones, but even she gives way to the dads and the older boys. Once when we complained about the lack of fans at our games, Ms. Cochran said, "All it takes is one championship season and you'll see them dying to get a look at you."

After he made a few shots, I felt my fingers begin to itch. It reminded me of the guy who taught dogs to start drooling whenever they heard a bell ring. Whenever I hear a basketball bounce, it makes me want to be out there dribbling. Finally, I couldn't contain myself anymore, so I blew my cover and walked onto the court. When he got a look at me, Dad stopped and just stood there bouncing the ball.

I said what Benny would have said. "Want to play a little one-on-one?"

He smiled. "You?"

"Sure. Why not?"

"Well, for one thing, I don't want to totally destroy your self-esteem." It felt good to hear him joke around. He sounded like the old Dad.

"Are you sure it would be mine that would get destroyed?"

He set the ball down and peeled off his shirt. His belly had a little pooch, but he was still in decent shape. "You're asking for it, you know."

"Maybe," I said. "Just toss it here."

He spun the ball to me and stood there with his hands on his hips. "Come on," he said. "You're going to regret this."

I gave a head fake to the left and then tried driving around him on the right. But my dad is like a big sequoia tree. And he's not only big, he's also quick. I thought I had him, but when I went up for the shot, the ball wasn't in my hand. It was back there with him. He just grinned and bounced it slowly.

"I thought you said you could play ball," he said.

Before I could answer, he took one step, set, and tossed a beauty that barely rattled the hoop. I took down the ball and sprinted back to the top of the key. We played for a few more minutes, but I didn't make one shot. And I didn't care a bit. Some parents let their kids shoot and win on purpose, but my dad isn't one of them. After his fifth steal he held the ball under his arm.

"I hear you're getting a new coach," he said.

"Do you know who it is?"

"Nope. But I mean, you know, come on . . ."

"Come on what?"

"It's the girls." I knew he was teasing me, and I loved it.

"You actually think the boys have a shot this year?" I said. The moment I said it, I wished I could take it back.

"Maybe," he said. But it was like someone had let the air out of a balloon. His head sagged, and he kicked at the concrete on the court.

I went on ahead anyway. "Want to take a bet on that one?" I asked.

He looked up. "Don't think so." He held the ball out in front of him and examined it.

"Dad?"

"Yeah?"

"You ready for another go?"

He smiled. "Wish I could. But if I don't get that work done your Mom keeps complaining about, I'll be raw hamburger tomorrow."

He bounced the ball to me, picked up his shirt, and walked off the court. I'd had to open my big mouth about the boys' team. I knew it reminded him of Benny. It's a curse to lose someone. When you start to feel good, you can forget about it for a while, but then you also forget the power that a single word can have.

I watched him walk away. I knew he missed Benny, but he never talked about it. I wondered if he even realized that I missed Benny too.

My mom was in the kitchen when I got back home.

"Where's Dad?" I said.

Mom handed me a glass of orange juice. "Probably at one of the Cones," she said.

"What was it you were wanting him to do around this place?"

"What are you talking about?"

"He said he had to come back home . . ." And then I got it. "Never mind," I said.

"Drink that," she insisted. "You need your vitamins."

"So do you."

She messed with her hair and sat down at the table. "I feel old," she said.

"You're not." I set down the glass and then went over and combed my fingers through her hair. My mom is beautiful, but not as beautiful as she used to be. Hearing the news about Benny took her looks away. She didn't care about makeup anymore, and she wasn't eating well, either. Her clothes seemed to hang off her now.

"Are you working later?" I asked. She had a part-time job at the Interstate Quik-Mart. She was really good with the customers, especially the ones who stopped off from the freeway. I had a dream once that she hopped into one of those people's cars and took off with them, never coming back. I think she might have had the same dream. Sometimes I caught a glimpse of it in her eyes. Maybe I wasn't the only one noticing cars from Montana.

"Yep. I've got ten till two. Can you handle it?"

"I suppose."

Up in my room I got out my homework and started reading, but after a while I couldn't see the words on the page anymore. I went across the hall to Benny's room. I left the light off and walked over by the window. I liked to see what his view of the world had been. Our side yard was lit up by the streetlight, but beyond that it was darker. I knew what the rest of the town looked like, and the hills with all the trees, but at night, when it was dark like this, I could imagine something different. A world far away and exotic. Maybe like the place where Benny was now.

I lay down on his bed. I could feel the impression his body had made in the mattress. It was like he was holding me, and I felt tears sting my eyes. It was so good to actually feel him around me, just like out on the playground. It wasn't the first time I wished I could see him, if just for a minute or two. If I could see and talk to my brother, I was certain it would make things better.

Benny was always the star of the family, but I never once minded. He was special, and people like that don't come along very often. Everyone from miles around came to his funeral. Boys from other teams dressed up in their letter jackets and wore their good shoes. They filled the church and lined up outside while my dad and the Schultzes and Darwin Ostrander and a couple of other guys from the '81 team carried Benny inside. You have to be special to have all that fuss made over you.

Part of it felt good. People were nice to me, coming over to tell me how sorry they were for my loss. People like Eric. While the boys stood together like crows on a phone line, he stepped over and took my hand.

"I'm so sorry for your loss," he said. Even the adults had noticed, especially his father and mine. But no one was going to say anything about a condolence at a funeral. Still, I always remembered and thought he was brave to have done it.

After the service everyone went to the Palm Café and told

stories about my brother, and after a while we started laughing. At a time like that you feel so sad, it almost seems wrong to laugh. But you don't realize then how hard it's going to be later, and how you need to take the laughter anytime you can get it.

I got up from Benny's bed and went to the closet. I pulled the string, and the light came on. On the floor was a big box full of his basketball stuff. I opened it and dug down inside. I found a pair of his favorite socks. Away-game socks: red and black. Lumberjack colors. They smelled like boys' shoes—not something you really want to be smelling much of. I slipped off my shoes and pulled on the socks. They went way up over my knees, but I didn't care. I turned off the light and went back to his bed. The socks felt soft and snug, like holding Benny close, and I made my decision right there. If anything was going to happen for me in basketball that year, having those socks on my feet would make the difference.

I heard the phone ring and then my mom yelled upstairs.

"Brenda! Phone!"

I took off the socks and put them back in the box. Downstairs, the phone was lying on the hall table.

"Who is it?" I asked Mom as she walked away.

"It's Mr. Hobbs."

"What does he want?"

"I didn't ask."

Mr. Hobbs had done some weird things before, but he'd never called my house.

"Brenda, my dear," he said, using his fake British accent, "is that you?"

"Yes, Mr. Hobbs. Did I miss an assignment?"

"For heaven's sake, no, my girl. I'm calling to tell you the good news."

"What good news?"

"I hear the muses calling, darling girl. And do you know what they're calling you?"

I was not prepared for the "darling girl" routine. "I don't know what you're talking about."

"Not to fret. I've been sent to interpret. Now, does the name Emily Dickinson mean anything to you?"

"Well, yeah. The poet, you mean?"

"Precisely. Quick, name one of her poems."

My mind went blank. "Mr. Hobbs . . ."

"Not to worry. I'm sure it's the stress of the moment. One will come to you. In the meantime, you're the first on the team to hear the good news. I've just come from the school board meeting and it's official."

"What's official?"

"That I've been named the new girls' head basketball coach."

"You've got to be kidding," I said. I obviously didn't hide my shock very well.

"It's the plain truth, my little Lumberjill. And the first meeting is Thursday night at my house. Will you be there, Miss Dickinson?"

"I . . ."

"Seven o'clock, and don't be late." He hung up the phone. And that's when I started dialing the rest of the team. The nightmare had begun.

# Chapter 5

News spreads like wildfire in Hemlock. Especially when it's as bad as a real wildfire. We were supposed to go to State this year. Didn't the school board understand that? Didn't anyone care?

"All I know," Jen said as we walked to school the next day, "is that if this was the boys' team, they'd practically be begging Michael Jordan to be the coach."

"Girls don't matter," Freddie said. "We all know that. How many girls' names do you see on the door of your dad's shop, Brenda?"

"It's a tradition," I said.

Freddie nodded. "Well, maybe it's not going to be that bad."

"Freddie," I said, "do I have to remind you about what's going on? What did he call you?"

"Edna. Can you believe it? Have you ever heard such a wretched name?"

"Yes," said Jen. "How about Vachel? God."

"I think he's finally lost his mind," I said. And I really thought he had.

Thursday night came and the three of us showed up together at the Hobbses' house. Mrs. Hobbs met us at the door. She dresses like a woman from the old days and has the kind of lap a kid would love to snuggle up in.

On the outside it looked like any other house in Hemlock, but the inside was how I imagined Mr. Hobbs's mind would look: a lot of clutter and books everywhere. There was a bookshelf in every room, with books falling off the shelves and spilling onto the floor. And perched on the couch was an embroidered pillow that said: IN THIS HOUSE THE DOG IS BOSS. It was hard to move around in such cramped quarters. Finally, all eleven of us found places to sit, and in came Mr. Hobbs.

I groaned. He was wearing the hat he always wears to our games. It's pink satin with a red-and-black hatchet on top made to look like it's stuck in his head. He thinks it's funny, but none of us ever laughs.

Mr. Hobbs jumped right in. "Ladies, ladies," he said. "How grateful I am to have you all here. And what a fine group of Lumberjills you are."

Jen pitched a fit. "Can we stop with the Lumberjill routine?" she said. "We're Lumberjacks."

"But you're ladies, Mr. Lindsay," he protested.

"Mr. Lindsay?"

"Yes, yes. Which brings me to the purpose of this meeting." He walked over to a makeshift podium made of plywood and stood behind it like a college professor. He picked up a couple of books and waved them. "This represents the secret to your success on the basketball court this year." He unfolded his wire-rim glasses and put them on his nose. Now he looked like Benjamin Franklin. "What do you suppose a team needs to have a successful season?"

"A real coach?" Jen asked.

"No," he said. "Teamwork."

"We have that," Freddie said. I thought she might spill it right then about the Napavine tree, but a quick look from Jen kept her mouth shut.

"Yes, but maybe not the right kind of teamwork."

I perked up at that one.

"You need the rhythm, the movement, the understanding that can only come from not paying attention."

"I've got that in math already," Freddie said.

"I don't get it," said Mavis. "We're not supposed to pay attention to the game?"

"That's exactly right, Robert. You don't pay attention to the game on, how shall I put this, on a conscious level. You're there and you're playing, but you're not there."

Jen jotted down a note and passed it to me. *He's lost his damn marbles,* it said. I passed one back. *He's scaring me. What are we going to do?*

I was waiting for Jen to write back when I suddenly realized it had gotten quiet.

"Emily?" said Mr. Hobbs. "Emily, are you paying attention?"

"Yes," I said. "I mean no. I mean, Emily?"

"What do you suppose was the earliest form of spiritual awakening for mankind?" he asked.

"Brad Pitt," Jen said.

I had to hand it to him. Mr. Hobbs hung in there. He rolled up his sleeves and leaned against the podium. "Think rhyme," he said.

42

"Poetry?" Lena tried.

"Exactly, Henry. Or something close to it. Imagine what early life must have been like with mankind as naked and vulnerable as we were. Why, at any moment we could have been snatched up by a saber-toothed tiger and served for dinner à la carte. Imagine how that must have made our souls bleed, made us wonder about the fleeting nature of life, made us appreciate the vicissitudes of love. Poetry sprang from these conditions, from those tortured souls."

"I still don't get it," Jen said.

"Here it is in a nutshell: Poetry comes from a different place in your brain."

"So?"

"And so does good basketball."

"Yes!" I said, more loudly than I meant to. But it was like a connection came together in my mind. It reminded me of Benny's advice about playing in the zone.

"I've given you all names, as you know. And some of you have voiced your displeasure, while others, as I can see, are still confused. Remember our starters from last year? Brenda, Freddie, Jen, and Mavis? Well, this year you will get to know them as Emily Dickinson, Edna St. Vincent Millay, Vachel Lindsay, and Robert Frost." He looked right at Lena. "We'll soon decide who the fifth starter is, eh, Mr. Longfellow? And the substitutes will include Mr. Shakespeare, Elizabeth Barrett Browning—oh, I love her, don't you all?"

He named the rest of the players while I sat there just shaking my head.

When Mr. Hobbs was through, Jen's hand shot up. "Is Vachel Lindsay a man or a woman?"

"A man. And a fine poet and performer. You would do

well to pay attention to the percussive image of 'The Congo.'"

But Jen shook her head. "There's no way I can be a guy."

"And I don't like the name Edna," Freddie piped in. "No offense to your mom, Tammy."

Mr. Hobbs held up his hands. "Ladies, ladies, we'll work out the problems as we go along, but for the time being I'm going to pass out your own personal poets so you can begin your study immediately. Your new basketball life begins now, and I'm here to tell you that if we can get this down, if we can become unconscious, there is no limit to what can be accomplished."

"Unconscious?" Lena asked.

"I'll explain later," said Mr. Hobbs.

"I wish I was unconscious now," Jen said.

"I wish I *were* unconscious," Mr. Hobbs corrected her.

"Whatever," she said.

Chapter

A few weeks later Mr. Hobbs took me aside in the hall at school and asked what I was going to do about college.

"I don't know," I said. "I'm thinking of Centralia Community."

I might as well have slapped him across the face. "Miss Dickinson, I am sorely disappointed in your selection."

"Well, it's not really a selection. It's just a place to go while I'm thinking about it."

He frowned and, like Santa, placed a finger at the side of his nose before he bent down, opened his briefcase, and pulled out a bunch of papers. "Now, I know we talked about this before, young lady. It sounds as if you haven't given it much more thought."

"Yes, I have," I said. "I thought about it. But you know, it's hard."

"The fact that no one in your family has ever gone to college," he said, "doesn't mean it's not possible for you. Here."

I took the papers from him. "What's this?"

"An application for the University of Washington. And if you need to know more, I can lend you a catalog."

"But—"

"Ah, I can see you might want more. Very well, here we go." He reached down again, and papers started bubbling out of his briefcase. "Let's see, Ivy League, the Seven Sisters, Whitman, Willamette. Are these more what you had in mind?"

"Mr. Hobbs, I don't know."

He kept on. "The University of Oregon, Cal Berkeley. I suggest you start knowing, Miss Dickinson, because very soon you may find representatives from these fine institutions knocking on your door asking for much more than just the time of day."

"Thanks," I said. "I'll talk to my parents about it."

He nodded. "Fine. But come talk to me as well," he said before continuing down the hall. I wasn't sure what he was talking about, but I liked his interest.

That night I was in my room with a book of Emily Dickinson's poems I'd picked up at the bookstore. I had mixed feelings about her poetry. About poetry in general, actually. It wasn't the kind of thing that was on everybody's tongue down at the Fir Cone or on the bus ride to an away game. Although Mr. Hobbs had chosen our poets for us, it was up to each of us to pick a poem to play by. From the looks of Emily Dickinson's work, there wasn't much to choose from. The woman was pretty depressed, and a lot of her poetry made me feel creepy. All that talk about death and sadness. I had hoped time was going to heal my pain about Benny. Why would I want to start thinking about dark things again?

But one poem really jumped out at me: "Because I Could Not Stop for Death." I kept going over and over the ones with bugs in the garden and other nature themes, but the book always fell open to "Because I Could Not Stop for Death." It was like I was getting a sign. Like somebody was looking over my shoulder and pointing a ghostly finger at that poem. So I chose it.

In bed that night I felt spooked for the first time since Benny's death. It wasn't a big rush, just a quiver in my heart. I rubbed at my chest to make it go away, and it did after a while. But in the middle of the night I woke up panting and with my heart skipping beats. I'd heard about that happening to old people, but it had never happened to me. I jumped out of bed and called my mom at work.

Mom has always had good parent radar. When I said hello to her, she immediately said, "What's wrong, Bren?"

"Nothing," I replied. But there was too big a pause. "Really, I'm okay."

"You don't sound right."

"I can't sleep is all. It's the poetry."

"Well, I told you Mr. Hobbs is a silly man sometimes."

"I know. It's just that . . ."

"Just what?"

"I'm feeling kind of nervous."

"Do you want me to come home, sweetie?"

"No, you don't have to do that. I just wanted to hear your voice."

"Is your father there?"

"I don't think so. I haven't heard him." Then the poem came back into my head. "Mom," I said, "does it ever get any better?"

She waited a few seconds. I probably shouldn't have asked her, but it was too late. "They say it does," she finally said. "You're thinking about your brother, aren't you?"

"A little. Do you?"

"All the time, Brenda. All the time." I could hear the break in her voice, and I wished I hadn't brought it up. The door buzzer went off in the background then, so I promised her I was fine and let her get back to work.

I put an extra blanket on my bed and then crawled under it. But there it was again. *Because I could not stop for Death, Because I could not stop for Death,* over and over again. It was gruesome, but so compelling. For a few minutes I tried to will it out of my head, and that finally worked. For the rest of the night my heart didn't do its little dance, but I was still shaky. I'm a strong, healthy person. Why was my heart acting like that?

The next day my dad had to go to a hearing in Chehalis at the Lewis County Courthouse, where he got a year's probation for tearing up the mill. He'd been making himself scarce around the house, so I'd been eating a lot of meals alone. Before going to work, my mom would leave plates of food in the fridge with little notes attached to them saying she loved me and wanted me to keep my strength up.

That night I'd just finished a plate of reheated lasagna when Jen called. "There's a rumor," she said.

"You want me to call the others?"

"I'm doing it," she said. "I'll meet you over there."

"Over there" was the City Hall. When I arrived, the boys' team was already milling around. Jen showed up with Freddie and Mavis, and a few minutes later Lena's mom dropped her off.

"What do you think?" she said to us. "You think it's true?"

"I wouldn't put it past them," said Jen.

"Where'd you hear it?" I asked.

"My cousin, Shana." Jen's cousin lived in Napavine. "She said everybody was talking about it."

I looked up at the tallest tree in Lewis County. Ever since we'd done the deed to the Napavine tree, there had been rumors that Napavine was after ours. The others kept talking about how and when Napavine might do it, but I found myself scanning the crowd.

"Looking for anyone in particular?" Jen whispered into my ear.

"No," I answered quickly.

"Well, he's looking at you."

"Who is?" I asked.

"Eric."

Across the parking lot Eric was standing alone. He was staring at me, so I waved at him. Then a car drove by, and we all turned to give it our meanest looks. It was a false alarm, just a couple more boys from our team. I thought Eric was going to talk to them, but instead he came over to us. "You think they're going to try to cut it down?" he asked me.

"You never know about them," I said.

"Of course they're going to try to cut it down," Jen said. "Why wouldn't they?"

But Eric didn't even look at her. "I'm sorry about the Hobbs thing," he said to me. "It's tough luck."

"He's not so bad," I said. "He means well."

It was bold of him to come over to us. I've heard boys say that walking into a group of girls is like throwing yourself into a volcano. And for a Jolley to walk over to a Jacobsen is even scarier. So when he started to fumble for something to say, I wanted to save him. But I couldn't think of anything.

"I better go," he finally said.

"Have a nice day," I said. I felt my face fire up.

When he walked back over to the guys, Jen turned to me. "'Have a nice day'? What are you, a McDonald's commercial?"

"He's a nice guy," I said. "I was just being friendly."

Most of the time Jen knows when to stop the teasing, and this was one of those times. She put her arm around my shoulder. "He's very cute," she whispered.

"He is," I agreed.

"I won't tell a soul," she said.

I guess that was my cue, because I unhooked myself from Jen and walked over to Eric. The boys stopped talking, and I realized I was on the brink of the volcano myself. "I'm not really a McDonald's commercial," I said.

Fortunately, he stepped away from the boys. "I wasn't thinking you were."

"I do want you to have a nice day," I stammered. "Or, well, I meant it, but not in the way it came out."

"I thought it was very poetic," he said with a smile. "So do you really think anybody's going to come and try to chop that thing down?"

I looked at the tree. "They might."

"How's your dad?" he asked.

"I don't know. I don't see him much. How about yours?"

"The same as ever. Maybe he's the one who should have

spent the night in jail instead of your dad. He was all Mr. Lecture that night. Learn to control yourself. Don't make a scene. If he only knew how much I'd like to make a scene once in a while."

"I can't picture you doing that," I said.

"What can you picture me doing?" He half smiled.

"Only good things, Eric."

He looked a little crestfallen, like he was expecting me to say something racier. But he recovered and said, "That's probably a compliment."

I wanted to talk longer, but the rest of the group started drifting closer and joined in, and soon both Eric and I were back talking to our friends. After a while I didn't want to be there anymore. This time, at least, our tree would have to be protected by someone else. I said goodbye to my friends and started walking. My hands were cold, so I put them in my pockets and took off down Main/56. I half expected the girls to follow me, but they didn't. I noticed the light was still on at my dad's shop, so I went to check it out. The front door was locked, but the inside was lit up. He and his friends sometimes hung out after hours, but I didn't see a soul in there.

I sat down on the front step and hugged my legs. Senior year wasn't turning out to be as different as I'd thought it would. I'd spent all my life waiting to get to this place, and frankly it was a letdown. I thought I would be a different person, but here I was, the same old Brenda. If Benny was still alive . . . I started to think. But I didn't want to spend the rest of my life beginning every sentence with "If Benny was still alive."

Benny. He always had a lot in common with our town and

our trees. He was like a tree himself. Sturdy with a lot of potential for growth. I guess I was always running under that tree for protection. During the bad times he'd be standing tall over me, so that only a few drops from the storm would trickle down through his branches. But there was no Benny now. Not many trees left at all, in fact. And no place for them to go with the mill closed.

What do you do when your protection is gone? People always say it's good to thin out a forest, because it lets the sun shine down on the smaller trees. Gives them strength to grow. So maybe I was out in the sun now. But when was I going to grow?

I stood up and started walking home. Hemlock seemed so quiet right now. No saws whining, no sawdust rattling in the chutes, no voices anywhere. Maybe change wasn't all bad. I felt peaceful, almost hopeful. The poem was out of my head. My heart was beating strongly. I could feel myself getting my basketball legs back. Maybe the mill would start up again. Maybe Mr. Hobbs knew what he was talking about after all.

Maybe.

# Chapter 7

Stan Schultz's prediction that the mill would open in two weeks did not come true, and things continued changing in Hemlock. The Palm Café closed during the week and now served dinner only on Friday and Saturday nights. The owner's wife went looking for work and found a job in Marys Corner at a feed store. All the women were waiting an extra couple of weeks to get their hair fixed, and the men put off oil changes for an additional thousand miles. There were a lot of leftovers in all the refrigerators. Around town everyone seemed to be looking a little older and walking a little slower.

October turned into November, and one day I went to Chehalis to pick up a prescription for my mom. On the way back I saw a truck parked in the Fostoria lot. Darwin Ostrander, our neighbor, was standing next to it, looking up at the smokestacks. He was wearing camouflage, but he stood out against the mill's gray metal siding. I pulled into the lot and parked next to him.

"Are you okay, Darwin?" I asked.

"You should touch it," he said. "Cold as ice, like there's no life left in her." He waved for me to follow him, and I did. His big work boots made deep impressions in the mud.

We walked over to the side of the plywood plant. He put the flat of his hand against the building and made me do the same. "Feel it?" he said.

When I was little, you didn't have to be right up next to the mill to feel it in your veins. It was your second heartbeat. It kept the sap running through you. Now it was still and the metal was ice cold. I pulled my hand back quickly.

"They ought to give her a decent burial," he said.

"You don't think it'll open again, Darwin?"

He looked at me seriously. "You're a smart kid. What do you think?"

I didn't want to say. It was like telling a town secret to someone from Napavine. "I'm hoping it will."

"Can I tell you something?" he asked.

"Sure."

"No, I mean if I tell you, you can't go telling anybody else."

"I won't."

"I talked to that lady."

"What lady?"

"The one from the county who was at the meeting that time. I told her I want to get retrained. I want to do something different."

"Like what?"

He was biting hard at his lip. "I've been suffering, Brenda. I've worked here for more than twenty years, and I've suffered every damn day. I've suffered right along with the poor trees."

Normally, Darwin was a good guy to be around, but this

side of him always made me nervous. When his wife died, he gave up for a while and was sent to the mental hospital in Steilacoom. When he came back, he was thinner and quieter. People avoided him when they saw him around town.

"You can hear them scream sometimes, Brenda. The trees, I mean. When the logs come in on the trucks, you can hear them. And they know when you put them on the belt that they're headed for the end."

"Oh, I don't know, Darwin."

"Everything that grows is alive," he said. "When you think about it, it's like Hemlock now. The company that owns this place just put us on the belt, and we're headed for the saw. Pretty soon you won't be able to recognize what's left of us."

"I don't want to think about things that way," I said. "Isn't there some hope?"

"You ask me, I think this town's headed for the end."

I decided to change the subject. "You never said what you wanted to do."

"I'd kind of like to be the sheriff of the woods. Work for the state and make sure everything is being taken care of."

"That sounds good," I said. "I think you'd be perfect for it."

"School starts in January," he said. "I'm going to be there."

"Good luck," I told him.

Then he said something funny. "Thanks, Brenda. And maybe you should start thinking about getting out while the getting's good too."

I don't know what I expected at our first practice, but I hoped it would at least have us playing something that resembled the game of basketball. Maybe it was a combination of having a new coach and getting over the embarrassment of acting like fools in front of one another. Whatever the reason, it didn't go well.

We were all changed and ready on time, shooting around in the gym while we waited for Mr. Hobbs. Ms. Cochran had always been an early bird, so it seemed strange right from the beginning. But when Mr. Hobbs finally showed up, strange took on a whole new meaning.

Usually a simple ensemble of gray sweats and sneakers will do for a coach. But not Mr. Hobbs. Is it possible to have a fashion sense that bad? I'd never seen a coach in neon yellow sweatpants and a lime green sweatshirt. That satin hatchet hat was perched on his head, and the whistle around his neck was the size of a bathtub faucet. His sneakers seemed too big for his feet and looked as if a kindergartner had used Magic Markers to paint them the school colors. When he walked across the floor, I saw our whole season run for cover.

"I don't get it," Jen said.

"Don't get what, Mr. Lindsay?" he asked.

"It," Jen repeated with a slight nod to his getup.

"I'm sure I have no idea what you mean," Mr. Hobbs said. "And might I ask what all you girls are doing standing around staring at me when you could be out there developing a raptor-sharp vision for the basket?"

As we shot the ball around, I recited my Emily Dickinson poem in my head. Lately it hadn't kept me awake at night, and it was nice to have it memorized. Mr. Hobbs said recitation would help us get our souls in shape, but try as I might, I didn't seem to be able to take it that seriously. I couldn't get the picture of my soul doing pushups out of my mind.

"Mr. Lindsay?" Mr. Hobbs called. "Have you got 'The Congo' memorized yet?"

"No," Jen replied.

"And might I ask why not?"

"It's an epic, Mr. Hobbs," she complained. "It'll take me the whole year."

"Well, if it takes you that long, I guess it will take you that long. But most of your learning time will be spent sitting on the bench."

Lena passed the ball to Jen and said, "I don't think you should memorize it anyway."

"Why not?" I said.

"Because it's a racist poem, and racism shouldn't be condoned by high school athletics."

The three of us stopped bouncing the balls and huddled up away from the others.

"What do you mean, racist?" Jen asked.

"Have you even looked at it, Jen? You should. Mr. Hobbs is right. It's very rhythmic and lyrically beautiful, but so what? It denigrates African people. Makes assumptions about their capabilities. Incorrect assumptions."

A big smile spread across Jen's face. "Mr. Hobbs!" she yelled.

I think the argument they had at that first practice really pepped things up. Mr. Hobbs loves a good debate, and it gave Jen something to fight about, which she loves. Then she practically mobbed Lena when Mr. Hobbs finally agreed about 'The Congo' and gave her more time to memorize a different Lindsay poem.

At the end of practice we usually spend time on the foul

line, perfecting our shots. But even this wasn't going to be easy. Mr. Hobbs had a so-called great idea that whenever we went up to the foul line, we should be bouncing the ball, reciting a line or two of our poem, bouncing the ball again, reciting another couple of lines, and then shooting the foul shot.

"It will keep those girls on the other team off-guard," Mr. Hobbs told us.

"It'll keep them laughing," said Jen.

But this was the first time we actually had to do it. When I went up to the line, I bounced the ball exactly three times, and then squeaked out:

> *"Because I could not stop for Death,*
> *He kindly stopped for me."*

Then a couple more bounces and:

> *"The carriage held but just ourselves*
> *And Immortality."*

Bounce-bounce, and then I took the shot. It ringed out.

"No, no, Miss Dickinson," Mr. Hobbs said. He was fumbling with the whistle at his lips and managed only to sound like an injured horse. "You've got to let them hear you."

I nodded and tried it again. *"Because I could not stop for Death . . ."* But then something snapped inside of me. The words forming in my head suddenly scattered in opposite directions. I tried to collect them, but they kept running away. I was having trouble catching my breath and went down on one knee.

"Miss Dickinson?" Mr. Hobbs said. "Miss Dickinson? Brenda?"

I heard voices around me, but they sounded hollow, like I was inside some kind of drum. I could feel my heart beating in my head, and sweat stung my eyes. I blinked to try to get rid of it, but all I saw were distorted faces: Jen's, Freddie's, and Mr. Hobbs's. I let them lay me down on the court. I looked up at the ceiling and saw big lights in metal cages, stained tiles, and a chain with nothing hanging from it.

I was breathing very fast, chugging along like a train, and there didn't seem to be anything I could do about it. My chest started to hurt.

"Bren?" It was Jen.

I wanted to calm her down, to tell her everything was okay, but somebody had glued my lips shut. The words started blending together and sounded like music played at the wrong speed. I kept staring at the ceiling until little by little it got all hazy and turned to black.

I woke up in the nurse's office. My mom was sitting in a chair at the foot of the cot I was lying on. The small lamp shining on the table next to her almost seemed to make her glow. She was looking up at the ceiling, and I could see her mouth moving.

"Mom?" I said. No more glue on my lips.

"Oh, my darling," she said. She practically fell off the chair getting to me. She started petting my head. "Oh, Bren, my little girl. When they called, I thought something bad had happened."

"Where is everybody?"

"The team's still out practicing. Do you want me to take you to the doctor? Does your head hurt?"

"No, nothing hurts. It was just weird. Everything stopped."

"Well, we're going to get you all checked over."

I didn't want that and told her so. "I'm fine," I said. "Really." My knees were wobbly when I stood up, but I didn't tell her. I just wanted to go home.

When we got there, I went up to my room and tried to do some homework, but I still felt a little shaky. Jen called and said she was putting together a petition to get Mr. Hobbs fired. It was nice to hear the support. Then Mom came in before she went to bed.

"What's Mr. Hobbs doing that has you girls all up in arms?" she asked.

I tried to explain as best I could, but I was tired of talking about it.

"Hold on a sec," Mom said, and she left for a few minutes. When she came back, she was holding her high school literature book. "I want to show you something."

She started leafing through the pages. "Here," she said, passing it to me. "I had Mr. Hobbs too."

"You did?"

"Yes—he was just starting out. And it doesn't sound like he's changed much. I didn't like him. But you know what? He got me so hooked on Dylan Thomas. This one especially. 'Do Not Go Gentle into That Good Night.' I loved that poem."

"You?"

"Don't act so surprised."

"Why this one?" I asked.

She took the book back and flipped the pages again. "I don't know. I liked what it had to say. *Rage, rage against the dying of the light.* I liked how mad he was. I liked how rebellious it made me feel. The whole idea of never giving up. You know, it made me shiver."

"Poetry made you shiver?"

"Well, this poem did."

"Somehow I can't see you doing that."

"I read it to your father before we were married."

"Dad put up with poetry?"

"Oh, he hated it. Hated Mr. Hobbs too. He said poetry was a waste of time. But we'd park out at Fostoria at night and I'd make him listen to it. We had big dreams then."

"Are you and Dad going to split up?" I asked.

She sighed. "I was hoping our little problems weren't that obvious."

"You're either yelling at each other all the time or doing the silent treatment. And he's hardly ever home anymore. It doesn't sound like little problems."

"Your father is having a hard time getting on with his life. When the mill opens again, he'll calm down. You'll see. But that isn't your concern now. You've got other things to think about." She put her hand on my forehead. "Are you feeling okay, honey? I'm worried about you."

It was useless talking about them, so I gave in. "I feel okay. I don't know what happened to me out there, but I'll be fine."

"Are you sure? I'm thinking we should run you to the doctor."

"I just don't know what to do about this poetry thing. It's embarrassing, and I don't see it helping."

"It helped me," she said. "Things weren't all that good in my life back then, and Dylan Thomas helped."

"What wasn't good about your life?"

She waited a second too long before she answered. "I don't know quite how to put this, because I don't know if you're feeling this way yet. But back then about all I had to look forward to was spending the rest of my life with Buzzy Jacobsen. Not that it was such a bad thing, but I couldn't help feeling there was something else, maybe something better, hiding inside me."

"What else could you have done?" I asked.

"I always thought it might have been a good idea to get out for a while. Before I settled in. You can always come back, but I don't think it's so easy to leave. Hemlock is a place that's too easy to settle into."

"What would you do if you could?"

"I'm not sure now. I've been thinking about school a little. Maybe my own business. I don't want to be making change at the Quik-Mart until I keel over."

I told her what Darwin said about the classes he was going to take.

"Even Darwin, huh? Seems like everybody's got change on their minds."

"I promised him I wouldn't tell anybody," I said.

"Don't worry," she said, patting my head. "I won't tell."

"What about Dad? What's he going to do?"

"Well, you know your father has always been a stubborn man. I suppose he'll wait for the mill to open until it or he crumbles to the ground from old age."

"And you'll wait with him?"

She reached over and touched my arm. "I don't know, Brenda. A few years ago I would have said yes. But now it doesn't seem the same anymore. I hope we make it."

"Me too," I said.

She grabbed on to my wrist, like maybe she thought I was falling away. "But for the time being, I've got you to be concerned about." She put her arms around me and held me close. "One good thing I got by staying here and marrying your father was you."

"And Benny," I reminded her.

I expected her to scold me for thinking that she might have left him out, but instead she only held me tighter and put her head on my shoulder.

"Mom, Mr. Hobbs thinks I should be applying to a bigger school. The University of Washington, maybe. I'm thinking about it."

She started shaking and then held herself in. Her eyes were red when she pulled away. "I hate the thought of you leaving," she said. "I know, I know, it's something you need to do. But I still hate it."

I held my mom again. I guess she wasn't just feeling sad about Benny. It was everything else too. The mill, her marriage, and maybe me. Eventually, she got up and left without saying good night. Sometimes she's off in her own world and doesn't realize it.

In bed that night I wondered if I was going off in my own world too. I'd never fainted before. Maybe there was something seriously wrong with me. I managed to drift off for a while, but something woke me and I sat up in bed. I must have still been asleep, because I said, "I know—I'll go ask Benny."

And I actually got up and went out in the hall before I caught myself. I stood there for a couple of minutes until my feet started getting cold.

"There is no Benny," I said. But I peeked in his door anyway, just to be sure.

Chapter 8

Over the next week Mom took me to the doctor and they did all kinds of tests and poked me with all kinds of needles. And what did they find? Nothing. If you're going to go through the pain, you should at least come up with something to make it worthwhile.

After I was cleared, I went back to school and to practice. It looked like it wasn't just me who'd been having problems. The team was a mess. One freshman girl had already quit. That left ten of us. Warming up, we looked like we were back in seventh grade. Lena made a good pass during a weave drill, but Freddie was in the wrong place and got smacked right in the side of the head. We knew how to do this perfectly, but our skills seemed to have disappeared.

We had the same plays as last year, but Mr. Hobbs wanted to name them differently. The UCLA play he now called Bloomsbury, and Duke became the Algonquin. Poor Jen. She was responsible for calling them out, and she almost started crying.

"Can't I just put up fingers for one, two, or three?" she yelled to Mr. Hobbs.

But he shook his head. "Your fingers mean nothing," he said. "Bloomsbury is everything."

"Four-point!" Jen yelled. "What's Bloomsbury?"

Lena stopped and cocked her head. "Bloomsbury was the name of an association of writers in England in the early part of the twentieth century."

Jen shook her head. "Come on, Mr. Hobbs. 'Bloomsbury is everything'?"

"And they were snobs," added Lena.

And so we progressed. With Lena's help we learned little-known facts about literary figures, none of whom had any possible connection to basketball. We memorized our poems for the foul line and recited them like shy grade-schoolers. All of us but Jen. She claimed she couldn't find the right Vachel Lindsay poem, but we all knew she was stalling.

I was nervous when I stepped to the foul line that first practice after passing out. I felt the blood pounding in my head again, and I thought for sure the same thing would happen. But it didn't. Emily Dickinson got her gruesome poem out without a hitch. I even sank six out of ten. Mr. Hobbs was happy about that, but we all left practice feeling like fools.

Mom had to work on Thanksgiving, so she stayed up late the night before and cooked the turkey and dressing for Dad and me. We ate it together on Thanksgiving Day in front of the TV. It was better than having to stare at the empty chairs at the dinner table. I'm not a fan of pro football, so I was only half watching, but Dad talked to the television every time a bad call was made. He knew the players by name and number. I think it takes dedication to know those details, but Mom says he just doesn't have enough to do.

I was finding it hard to talk to my dad. We hadn't really said much to each other since the day at the playground. And I'd noticed he was starting to look different. He wasn't shaving every day anymore, and he'd wear the same clothes a few days in a row. He was like that right after Benny died, but I thought he'd gotten over it.

I cut him a piece of pie, and he ate it without taking his eyes off the screen. At a commercial I decided to ask him something.

"Mom says she read poetry to you when you guys were going out."

"Yeah, I guess," he said.

"Did you like it?"

"No, not really." His eyes were still on the TV. "That Hobbs was a freak."

"He still is," I said. "Did you know we started practice?"

"That's what Mom said. How's it going?"

"Weird." I told him about the poets.

"Yeah, I heard about it," he said. "Some people aren't very happy."

"Really? Who?"

He shrugged. "You know. Some people. They say he hasn't got any business coaching. I'll say one thing. If he doesn't shape up, that guy better watch his back."

I didn't like the sound of that. I picked up the plates and put them in the kitchen. When I came back, the game was on again and Dad was spread out on the couch.

"I'll bet you're happy basketball's about to start," I tried.

"Not really," he said.

"But you love basketball."

He finally looked away from the TV and stared me down. "Not anymore, I don't," he said.

That was about as plain as my dad was going to get. I stayed there a few minutes longer, trying to think of something more to say. All I could come up with was "Do you want anything else?" But he shook his head, so I left the room.

I stood in the kitchen and looked out at our driveway. The old hoop was hanging off the garage, and the mist in the air was sifting through the net. If Benny had still been alive, he and I would have been out there shooting. The sound of the bouncing ball would have brought my dad out, and Mom would have been looking through the window instead of me. I'd have waved to her and she'd have broken into that terrific smile that said, "I just love my family."

Now the hoop looked lonely, as if it yearned for better times. I wanted to go into the living room, yank Dad off the couch, and make him play a game of one-on-one. Even if it hurt when he drove past me, even if I never got off a single shot. Those are the types of pain you can live with.

The first game of the season was on December 1 at Boistfort. It was a Friday-night away game. I've always liked away games, because we get out of school early and take a long bus ride, which helps me focus.

But I felt fidgety on that trip and sat way in the front of the bus, with the underclassmen. Seniors usually sat in the back, spelling words backward on the frosty windows, talking about boys, or making up ways to bug the younger players.

I'd waited three years to do that, and here I was, not really caring. The rest of the seniors didn't seem to mind. Jen was spelling up a storm in the back and keeping them all entertained.

But I was nervous about the game. During practice I'd been adjusting to saying my poem at the foul line. No more passing out, but I still had some stage fright about it. I had images of the whole gym breaking into hysterical laughter if I said, *"Because I could not Death for stop."* The other girls were feeling the same way, especially Jen. She'd finally settled on a Lindsay poem, but she said it so softly, we couldn't really hear it. Even Mr. Hobbs couldn't coax it out of her. Would we be the laughingstock of the league? The whole state, maybe?

The preseason poll in the Tacoma newspaper had us ranked tenth in the state, but that was based on last year and the players we had coming back. They hadn't interviewed Mr. Hobbs, and I'm sure they weren't aware of what was going on down in Hemlock. If they were, I don't think you'd have seen our name on any list of best teams.

The trouble was we just weren't jelling. We all knew how to play well, but we were still running into one another, trying to bounce balls so they made a kind of rhythm, throwing ourselves around in frustration, and generally threatening to kill one another. Another freshman quit, which brought us down to nine, and Jen was making serious noise about hanging it up herself. During the last practice before our first game, Mr. Hobbs had announced that Lena was going to start, but even that thrill was short-lived. What had happened to the red-and-black machine we once were?

My mom was already at the gym when we got there. She'd

surrounded herself with her coat, a Diet Pepsi, and a couple of paper bags that I knew had homemade popcorn and other snacks inside. Some of the boys' mothers were camped around her, but my dad was nowhere to be seen. Girls' games were usually played first, so the men who followed the Western Lewis County League mostly caught the tail ends of our games while they waited for the boys to start.

I waved at Mom as we walked in, and she blew me a kiss. I think the start of the basketball season was taking her mind off her troubles, because she looked like a high school girl herself up there in the bleachers, happy and excited. Sometimes it's hard to imagine your own parents when they were your age. Especially reading poetry to each other. But while I dressed in the locker room, I thought about what my parents' dreams might have been. Mom kept telling me that dreams back then weren't the same as dreams now. Sometimes I wondered if it was possible that all the dreams had been used up. It seemed like I'd had some at one time, but since Benny's death they'd gone someplace else. Maybe it doesn't get you anywhere to dream. My mom had had dreams, and look where they'd gotten her. She'd placed her bets on my dad, and here they were, on the verge of calling it quits.

The locker room was quiet. All of us seemed to be thinking the same thing: We wished the game was over and we were home in our beds with the covers up over our heads. But I had my little secret in my gym bag, and when Freddie and Jen moved away, I pulled it out. I put Benny's game socks on over mine, and as soon as they were on, I felt more strength in my legs. When I stood up, I practically bounced around the room.

Mr. Hobbs knocked on the locker room door and asked if we were all decent. That's the problem with having a male coach—he can't be in there with you while you get ready for the game. Jen glanced over to me and I saw the wary look in her eyes. Freddie had it too. It said, "Are we really going through with this?" But at this point we had no other choice.

"Now, girls," Mr. Hobbs began after we let him in.

But none of us was paying attention, because he had that hat on. There he was dressed in a nice normal suit, but the hat was enough to make us mute.

"I know you're all probably as nervous as cats tonight, this being your first game and all, but I have total and complete confidence in you. You were born to play and bred to win. Hemlock is lucky to have you girls representing it."

"I'm not feeling so hot," Freddie said. She had forgotten to tie one of her shoes.

"You will begin feeling hot when the competition stares you in the face," Mr. Hobbs said. "Now, do we all have our assignments? We have Miss Dickinson, Mr. Frost, Mr. Longfellow, Mr. Lindsay, and Miss Millay starting tonight. But the rest of you—you there, Mr. Blake—you need to be ready to be called. Mr. Lindsay, have you gotten your foul line down?"

Jen frowned but nodded.

"Is something wrong, Mr. Longfellow?"

We all turned and looked at Lena. The normally calm, self-secure brainiac looked pasty and was chewing on her lip. "No," she managed to squeak out.

"Are you sure?"

She nodded.

"Well, maybe a short recitation will calm your nerves."

We groaned, as if all nine of us had a toothache at the same time.

"Mr. Longfellow?"

*"The day is, uh, the day is . . ."*

"Yes, yes, *The day is done . . ."*

"That's right," Lena said. *"The day is done, and the darkness Falls from the birds of Night . . ."*

"Mr. Longfellow? The *birds* of Night? Come now. Is that the language of the gods?"

Lena's shoulders drooped like a wilting flower.

"Oh, for God's sake!" Freddie shouted. "Come on, Fourpoint. *The day is done, and the darkness Falls from the* wings *of Night.* Geez."

At that, Lena jumped up and ran to the back of the locker room, where Mr. Hobbs couldn't go.

He scratched at his hat. "I fear we have some work to do," he said.

One of the younger girls got up and searched Lena out while Mr. Hobbs lined up the rest of us and began pacing. He stopped and looked at us, like an artist in front of his canvas. "Ah," he said. *"Whenas in silks my Lumberjills go."*

By the time the game started, the bleachers were about a quarter full. The Boistfort girls were a gum-snapping, loud-talking, elbow-slashing group of loggers' daughters who didn't like us being on their court. But I think they relaxed a little when they saw us come out with our coach. After all, Mr. Hobbs was still wearing that ridiculous hat. He proudly stepped onto the court and shook each of our hands when the eighth-grade kid announced the starters.

I was in the circle for the opening jump. I looked at my team gathered around, saw the panic on their faces, and said a little prayer before the whistle blew. Then we were off.

I won the tip-off, and it felt right at first to have the ball in my hands. Exciting, like shaking a wrapped package at Christmas. I tossed the ball to Jen, and she shouted, "Bloomsbury!"

We quickly set up for the play, but a Boistfort player intercepted a pass, so we ran to the other end and set up on defense.

It all might have gone according to plan if Mr. Hobbs hadn't started to drown out everybody in the place.

"Get her!" he yelled like machine-gun fire. "Get-her-get-her-get-her."

I heard the laughter in the stands.

He stood and paced the bench. "Get thee out of the key!" he screamed. "Forsooth, she stands ankle deep in that mire!"

A coach just doesn't say things like that in the heat of battle. Forsooth? The refs both smiled around their whistles.

The idea was to blend together unconsciously, but all I saw was a whole lot of conscious for the first part of the game. Boistfort had a good outside shooter, and she hit three in a row. Meanwhile, Freddie, our own brilliant shooter, was in a dribbling frenzy. While normally she could get around nearly any defender and lay up some beauties against the backboard, all she did that game was dribble. Even when she had a clear lane to the basket, she'd suddenly turn and dribble back out and pass to someone else. And that someone was usually me. That's why I scored so much early on. Whenever I had a clear path to the basket, I moved in to bang one off the backboard.

Unfortunately, their tall girl caught on and finally took the opportunity to smack me on the arm. So I was the first to go up to the foul line.

It was my intention to walk up to the line, aim, and fire up my shots. But before I had the chance, I heard Mr. Hobbs from the sideline.

"Miss Dickinson," he warned.

I looked at him and then up a few rows at my mother. Then I bounced the ball before I whispered, *"Because I could not stop for Death."* I threw up the shot and made it. My mom cheered. The Boistfort girls, lined up on either side of the key, wrinkled their foreheads.

Second shot. Bounce-bounce.

"Louder, Miss Dickinson," Mr. Hobbs said.

I really tried. *"He kindly stopped for me."*

I heard the other girls whisper, heard more of a murmur in the crowd. I put up the shot, and it clanged off the rim. Boistfort cleared it and I trotted by our bench, frowning at Mr. Hobbs. But he had his hands out, clapping.

"Excellent," he said.

I don't know how we did it, but we made it through the first half and were down by only three points. With the way we were playing, the game should have been all over by then. As we trudged toward the locker room, I saw more people coming into the gym. A little boy pointed at me as I walked by. "She's the one," he said. "She's the one who talks when she shoots."

In the locker room Mr. Hobbs was not happy. "What is the problem?" he asked us.

I'm not normally a complainer, so I waited for the others to explain, but they kept their lips pressed tightly together.

"The only one contributing out there is Miss Dickinson," Mr. Hobbs said. "Let's take advantage of our opportunities."

When we came back out, I was shocked to see the stands were packed. Was it that good a game? It was great to have a crowd, but it didn't help. Three minutes into the second half we were already down by ten.

And it was soon clear why everyone had decided to come into the gym. They wanted to know what all the fuss was about the Hemlock girls and to see Mr. Hobbs make a fool of himself. Mr. Hobbs entertained them as best he could. At one point he even quoted from "The Raven" when the refs made a bad call.

"Nevermore!" he shouted.

The boys in the Boistfort section fell over themselves laughing, and shouted back, "Nevermore!"

On one trip down the court, I saw my dad come into the gym with the Schultz twins. He leaned against the wall with his arms crossed and had that look on his face that told me he and Jim Beam had been spending too much time together that day. But it still felt good to see him there.

We kept up as best we could during the second half, but it wasn't us out there. Mavis was taking wild shots completely outside the three-point line when she wasn't even being guarded under the basket. Freddie kept up with her dribbling show, and whenever Lena got the ball, she froze and just stood there. I don't know how many times Boistfort managed to steal the ball from her, but it might have been a Western Lewis County League record. Even Jen, the daring playmaker on our team, held the ball only a couple of seconds before passing it off to me. In fact, everybody was passing the ball my way. I was beginning to think they wanted to make a star out of me in the very first game.

I guess I came through for them. My deadeye baseline jumper was going in, and I was the only one driving to the basket. I was piling up the points. When I'm doing well in a game, I feel like I can do no wrong. I took chances, one time stealing the ball and running the length of the court to lay up a beautiful basket right in front of my dad. I really wanted to do well with him watching.

With about four minutes left, the game was tied. I stole the ball on an inbound pass and tried to put it up. Unfortunately, the tall girl fouled me again, and there I was, at the line, with the fans as quiet as could be, just waiting. I could almost feel them all leaning forward in the bleachers. I bounced the ball for a long time, so long that the ref nodded for me to shoot.

*"Because I could not stop for Death."* I shot the ball and made it.

But just as the ball went through the net, I heard my dad say, "What the hell?"

The crowd started buzzing while the ref retrieved the ball and handed it back to me.

*"He kindly stopped for me."* Bounce-bounce. *"The carriage held but just ourselves."* Bounce-bounce. *"And Immortality."* I quickly put it up, but the ball clinked off the rim and Boistfort got the rebound.

They drove to the other end and made a basket, putting us behind by one. Jen brought the ball down, but the same thing happened again. The closer she got to the defenders, the more like a scared rabbit she became. She dribbled ahead a few steps and retreated. Then she passed it to Freddie, who dribbled from one side of the court to the other.

"Miss Millay!" Mr. Hobbs shouted.

But Freddie ignored him and passed to me. I sank a jumper and we were back on top.

Boistfort called a timeout, and we went into a huddle.

Mr. Hobbs's face was bright red. "Girls," he said, "I urge you to come out of your reverie and join this battle."

But we were distracted. Something big was going on under our basket.

"Oh, my God," Jen whispered to me. "It's your dad."

I turned and saw my dad on the court holding the game ball under his arm. Both refs were in front of him; one had her hand out.

"Give it to me," she said.

But Dad held it firm. "What the hell kind of joke is this game?" he said.

"Ignore them, please," Mr. Hobbs said to us. "This contest is about to slip from our grasp."

But I couldn't ignore them. It was my dad out there on the court. The Boistfort fans were loving it. They were shouting at my dad, egging him on. But when I glanced up at my mom, she definitely wasn't smiling.

"Who says a damn poem on the foul line?" Dad shouted. Then he looked right at me, and I could see his disappointment. He didn't have to say anything more. I could hear him in my head: "Benny would never do this sort of thing." I turned back to the huddle while the refs closed in on my dad.

"You must forsake the call of the angels on your shoulders and give these other girls the devil in return," Mr. Hobbs said. "You can do it."

But it was hard to listen. When we broke to resume the game, a couple of security guys were hauling my dad out of the gym. He was cursing and yelling all the way through the doors.

I suppose it was seeing my dad being dragged off that changed my game. In those last few minutes the basket had a lid on it. Nothing I put up managed to make it through. And now it was Boistfort that could do no wrong.

I couldn't stand it. When the horn sounded to end the game, we'd lost, 64–59. In the locker room I picked up a towel and sat down hard on the bench. Our first game of the season and we were already on a losing streak. I draped the towel over my head and stared down at my shoes. My feet were throbbing. Maybe it was a message from Benny. Maybe he was trying to work those socks off my feet and onto someone who deserved them more.

# Chapter 9

I sat by myself on the bus ride home. Not that I had much choice. Mavis and Freddie sat in the back in one seat, and Jen and Lena were across the aisle. Nobody was saying much of anything, and it actually felt good to be alone for a while.

About halfway home, though, I couldn't get the game out of my head, so I turned around and stared at Jen until she caught my eye. I wouldn't look away, so it wasn't long before she caved in and walked up to where I was sitting.

"What's the deal?" I asked. "How many points did you score? Three?"

"Five," she said.

"You average fifteen."

"So it was a bad game. Sometimes it happens. You shouldn't complain. Thirty-three points is pretty darn good."

"Yeah, well, I feel like I stole some from you guys. Did you see Freddie? What was going on with her?"

Jen didn't say anything. She turned around and looked to the other girls, as if for an answer.

"Jen?" I asked.

"Oh, all right," she said, turning back with a fit-to-kill look on her face. "There was no way I was going to let myself get fouled by those Boistfort girls, Bren. No way I was going up to the line and getting razzed by the fans."

Then it dawned on me. "You mean?"

"It wasn't anything we all got together about, nothing like that. It just sort of happened."

I slumped in my seat. "Great. You didn't want to be the freak show, but you were willing to let me do it."

"I can't speak in front of crowds." It was Freddie sneaking up the aisle. Behind her were Mavis and Lena. "You know I freeze up."

"What's got into you all?" I asked. "We probably lost the game because you were too chicken."

"You were great, though," said Mavis.

"Well, we might as well turn in our jerseys," I said. "Looks like the season's already over."

"Maybe we should boycott," said Freddie.

"From the looks of it, you guys already have," I said. "Listen, I heard a lot of people complaining about the game. Maybe we don't have to do anything. Maybe he'll get fired or something. But next time I wish you would include me in your little plan."

"Okay, okay," Jen said. "We get it. Now, come on back and sit with us."

I did. I guess you can't complain about a team not acting like a team if you're going to pretend you're not a part of it. So

I crowded in the back with them and we talked about the game all the way back to Hemlock.

Jen drove me home from the bus garage. We passed by the mill on the way, and we both glanced over to look. It was so dark, I could barely make it out, but I knew it was there. I remembered feeling the cold side of it with Darwin Ostrander.

It was starting to rain when Jen dropped me off at my house. There was a note from Mom on the kitchen table:

Have an errand to run. I'll be back soon. Beautiful game, my darling. There's a plate of chili mac in the fridge. Put it in the microwave and run it for two minutes. M.

I guess she thinks the microwave is a complicated appliance. Sometimes she forgets I'm seventeen.

I was just about finished eating when she got home.

"Great game, honey," she said, hugging me. "Did you like the casserole?"

I nodded and put my plate in the sink. "We lost."

"Yes, but you played so well."

"What happened with Dad?" I asked. "Is he in jail again?"

"No, he's not in jail. But he might as well be." She walked out of the room.

When I caught up with her, she had her old English lit book out and was sitting on the couch.

"Where is he?" I asked.

"At the shop."

"This late?"

She was leafing through the book but stopped to look up at me. "He's an adult, Brenda. He makes his own decisions." She looked down at the book again. "I'm just trying to figure out what this means."

"They had to drag him out of the gym," I said. "Why would he do something like that?"

"Ah, here it is. Now, let me read this to you, Brenda, and tell me what you think." She started reading the Dylan Thomas poem.

"Mom!"

She looked up and I could see tears on her face. "I told him not to come home, honey," she said.

"That was the errand you had to run?"

"Yes. I've had enough. I can't take any more of this behavior."

I was stunned. "But Mom."

"I won't stand for it," she said. "You saw what he did at that game. Is that what you want to look forward to every time you play? Does it help you focus when you have to worry about what your father's going to be up to? You shouldn't have to think about that."

"But what are we going to do?" I asked.

"That's a good question. Not that life isn't pretty lousy these days anyway. But we'll just make do, Bren. We'll make do."

"So he's going to live at the shop?"

"There's that little apartment in back. He'll be fine."

I sat on the other end of the couch. "It's just not fair," I said. "Everything used to be good, and now it all seems so bad."

"It wasn't all good, Brenda."

"But ever since Benny, things aren't going right."

"Don't blame your brother," she said.

"I'm not."

She looked at the book again. *"Rage, rage against the dying of the light,"* she whispered.

I was so tired, I went upstairs to bed. I didn't feel rage, exactly, but I definitely was mad at my mom and my dad. I went to sleep wondering when they were going to grow up. And when it was that I had become the adult.

So it looked like Mom wasn't going to go gentle into that good night after all. Even though Dad hadn't been around much lately, I found myself missing him. That night I woke up every couple of hours, wondering what he was up to.

On Sunday I got a call from Jen. "I am definitely quitting the team," she said. Then she started crying. I knew it was hard for her to get those words out. Jen had spent her whole life working to be the best. She has a complex about herself, and she thinks she's not good at anything. It's a mystery to me how that happens. They were going to put psychology on our senior schedules but decided at the last minute that it wasn't important enough. I wasn't so sure. When the mill shuts down and your favorite coach leaves and your brother dies, it seems like a good idea to put it back in the plan.

I went over to Jen's house. We sat in her basement, watched TV, and shared a bottle of Diet Pepsi. Jen's eyes were all red and runny and she clutched a wad of Kleenex in her hand, but I just waited for her to bring it up.

"There's no way I'm going out on that floor again," she finally said. "It's over."

"Come on, Jen. You're just mad because we lost."

"But did you hear the people in the crowd?"

"Yes, I did. In fact, I was the only one who had to stand up there and listen to them, thanks to you all."

"It was just too embarrassing. I can't do it."

"Well, my dad didn't help much," I said. I told her his punishment: He'd been banned from all gyms in the Western Lewis County League for the rest of the season.

"That seems harsh," she said.

"It could have been worse. You know what he's like when he drinks too much."

"Yeah. But I've always liked your dad. He's funny."

"Try being his daughter," I said.

We watched the soda fizz in the bottle. "So you're going to keep practicing?" Jen asked.

"Yes."

"Why? It's over. Don't you think?"

"Because I turned out. Because you have to finish what you start. Maybe Mr. Hobbs will see his ideas are wrong and we'll get back to playing real basketball."

She was quiet for a while, so we pretended to watch an ad for wrinkle cream on the TV.

"Bren, do you think I could play at a higher level?"

"You mean can you get better?"

"No, I mean, after high school. Do you think I could play ball at college?"

"Of course I do. Who shoots a running jumper better than you?"

"Well, you do for one. I think I'm too short."

"You're too short to play center, but after that it's wide open. You can't play at college if you don't play this year, though."

"Maybe you're right. Maybe Mr. Hobbs will change his mind. How'd you feel standing up at the line saying those things?"

"Stupid."

"Didn't you just want to curl up and die?"

"Not quite."

She was quiet for a moment. "I'm sorry, Bren," she said. "I didn't mean anything by that."

"Stop doing that. Quit apologizing."

"Okay, I will," she promised. "I'll try."

We watched another commercial, this time for beer. That's something we didn't need any more of in Hemlock. We laughed about what the Schultz twins would look like doing a reality commercial in front of the Cones. It relaxed us, made us forget about the team for a while.

"So," said Jen, "what's the deal with you and Eric?"

That took me by surprise. "Eric Jolley?"

"The one and only. I mean, he walked up to you the other day at the tree. And I noticed he wasn't talking to anyone else."

"He's just a decent guy, Jen. That's all."

"But what's going on? He's never done that before, has he?"

I told her about the night at the mill. "He was really nice to me," I said. Then I remembered Benny's funeral. "And he seems different than most of the guys in this town."

"Well, I was just wondering is all," she said. "It seems funny you would be interested in a Jolley."

It got me thinking after I left Jen's house. My father didn't like the Jolleys and never had. In fact, my grandfather hadn't liked them, either. Mr. Hobbs once made us write a report about our ancestors. I found out that my own ancestor, Ira Jacobsen, cleared the whole area so they could plan it out for a town. And guess who was the town planner: Tensed Jolley. That was the beginning of the feud; something to do with

Tensed Jolley following Ira Jacobsen around telling him which tree stumps to pull out and where he wanted his spectacular house to be built. Kind of a master-servant relationship, I guess. And maybe it's still like that. I've heard Dad call Lester Jolley a slave driver and an overseer. But Eric didn't seem like that to me. He seemed kind and gentle, not interested in the history between our families.

I should have gone home right then, but I didn't. Home had a different feel to it now. Instead, I walked along Main/56. Hemlock still seemed to be taking a big nap. The video place was humming, but the Palm Café and Maida's were locked up tight. Of course, the Pine Cone and the Fir Cone were open for business. I guess when times are tough, people still like to gather and drink. I caught the familiar smell of the Fir Cone as I walked by: a mixture of cigarette smoke, spilled beer, and toilet cakes. It was a sad smell. The town seemed as depressed as some of the people in it. I stopped to pick up a plastic bag and carried it until I found a trash can. Maybe Hemlock needed some help taking care of itself.

I wound up at the Jacobsen Barber Emporium. The front door was open even though it was pretty nippy outside. As I went in, I checked out the names on the doorjamb.

All the big players from Hemlock's sports history were listed. My dad was there. A Schultz from way far back. Benny. It was crowded with old pencil marks. All boys. One name was even carved by a knife, with a chunk of wood missing as if to prove a point. Before, I hadn't minded, but now seeing only boys' names bothered me. Where in this town could the women's tradition be carved out?

I stepped inside. I heard noises, so I went through the shop

85

and leaned against the doorway to the back apartment. There I found my dad lying on the couch. He was still in his bathrobe, watching a video with his feet up.

The video was a combination of shots from Benny's games. If you didn't know better, you'd think Benny had scored a thousand points a game, that he'd never made mistakes, that he'd been the most magical dribbler who ever hit the court. Even the title my dad had put on the box told it all: *Best of Benny*. I quietly slid my back down the doorjamb and watched.

No matter how much time passes, no matter how many times I tell myself I'm over it, I'll never get used to the fact that I can watch my brother play his heart out on tape and at the same time know that he'll never pick up a basketball again. Why do we invent things like pictures and videos that fool us into believing people can go on forever? Do we do it just to torture ourselves? But at the same time I was hypnotized watching the screen.

Some of the shots were from when Benny was in middle school, and they didn't look as professionally made as the later ones. My mom used to hold the camera a lot, because the games had conflicted with Dad's work schedule at the mill. The scenes were a little jumpy, but they had the same effect. There was Benny, looking like puberty was never going to visit him.

But as the tape moved along, I noticed a voice cheering in the background. It made my throat tight. It was my own voice that I was hearing, that Dad was hearing. Back then I always sat next to my mom at Benny's games, and I was his best cheerleader. I whooped and hollered even after the play was made, so much sometimes that my mom had shushed me.

I guess she thought that if she finally put me on camera, I'd calm down. So there I was looking like a freak. My hair was chopped as if they'd put a bowl on my head and cut around the rim, and I had a huge smile, my teeth still too big for my mouth.

"What do you think about your brother?" my mom was asking on the tape.

"He's just the best, of course," I was saying. "Really the best."

I heard my dad laugh at that. Then he shook his head. He fast-forwarded to a more recent game and wiggled his bare toes.

I stood quietly. I wanted to walk in and plop myself down next to my dad. I wanted the two of us to curl up together and watch our son and brother do what came to him so naturally. I felt it in my bones. They actually ached for my brother. I hardly talked to anyone about Benny because, if I did, I usually ended up crying. But now not talking about him didn't seem right, either. I felt as if I was already forgetting him.

"Benny, I want to see you again, " I whispered, too softly for my dad to hear.

There's an old saying I should have paid attention to that night: Be careful what you wish for, because you just might get it. The real craziness was about to begin.

# Chapter 10

It began at the first practice after the Boistfort loss. None of us was in a very good mood. I'd convinced Jen not to quit until we could talk to Mr. Hobbs, but I was nervous because I wasn't sure how he would respond. A lot of people had been talking about him, and most of it wasn't very positive.

We all got dressed and went up to our half of the gym. Mr. Hobbs was already there shooting baskets. He'd toned down his outfit, but he still wore the hat. Some people just can't take a hint. While the nine of us started stretching, he walked around, talking about the game.

"Now, if we had only stayed on course, we could have won that game," he said. "Despite the unfortunate circumstances, we still could have pulled it out."

By rights it should have been me who said something, but Jen straightened up and took him head on. "What's that supposed to mean?" she asked.

"Well, if we had stuck to the plan."

"No, I mean 'unfortunate circumstances.' What does that mean?"

Mr. Hobbs glanced at me and tried to steer the talk in another direction. "The circumstances that were out of our control."

"He was just doing what any normal dad would have done," Jen said. "He saw what kind of bull it all was."

"Now, Mr. Lindsay," Mr. Hobbs tried.

"No, really," she kept on. "Don't you get it? Nobody thinks this poetry thing is a good idea. Nobody. You take a poll out there, and you'll find ninety percent of the people in this town think you've gone cuckoo."

My stomach started to grind as I listened to her. Jen had always spoken her mind, but Mr. Hobbs wasn't really the type of guy who could take much of what she was dishing out.

"Any new plan takes time to kick in," he said.

She stared at him for a second and then shook her head. "You poor pathetic dude. That's it. I'm out of here." Jen glanced at me as she passed, even bumped my shoulder. I guess it was a signal for me to follow, but I couldn't.

"Anyone else feel that way?" Mr. Hobbs asked. "Anyone else want to hop off the train before it even leaves the station?"

No one seemed to be grabbing the bait. Jen stopped at the bleachers and took one last look before she disappeared.

My stomach was an empty pit. Without Jen, there was no way we'd ever get very far as a team. She was our glue. If Mr. Hobbs had thought we weren't cohesive before, wait until he saw us without Jen.

"Well, this isn't a particularly good omen," he said. "Does anyone else have anything to say?"

"She's embarrassed," I said. "We're all embarrassed, Mr. Hobbs."

"Embarrassed? About what?"

"Having to stand at the line and recite poetry. It's just asking for trouble. You heard the kids in the stands."

"Well, first of all, from what I could decipher, you're the only one who can actually say what it felt like, since no one else had the wherewithal to get to the line. And secondly, Miss Dickinson, you of all people should know it's not about the people in the stands. They're just envious of you. They all wish they could be out there doing what you do."

"Nuh-uh," Mavis said. "Not one of them wants to be out there reciting poetry."

The rest of the practice was a disaster. Jen didn't come back, so Freddie and I were left to try to direct things. But it didn't work without Jen, and Mr. Hobbs knew it. He finally told us to go shower and we'd try again the next night.

There was a lot of grumbling in the locker room. Jen's locker was hanging open, and most of her stuff was gone. It looked like she meant business.

I stayed there for a while after everyone left. I felt tired and shivery, and my stomach was really starting to hurt. I wanted to cry but swallowed it down. At times like this I used to go into Benny's room and hang out with him. He wasn't much for figuring things out directly. He liked talking about sports and food and other kids at school, but somehow that helped. He could go at a problem from a different angle so the problem looked smaller. I wanted so much to talk to him about every-thing. Just five minutes was all I needed. I knew he would have had something helpful to say.

While I thought, my hands made fists and I felt as if I had electricity circulating through my veins. I swallowed hard again, but a lump swelled in my throat. I felt panic rising from nowhere. And then a voice:

"I suppose you're going to blame me for all this, aren't you?"

I spun around, nearly toppling off the bench. But I was still alone. At least I thought I was. My heart was chugging at top speed.

"Up here," the voice said.

And then I saw him. My brother, Benny, was sitting on top of one of the lockers, kicking his feet against the metal. I stood up fast. My whole body was vibrating.

"If you ask me," he said, "Jen's just jealous because you're a better poet than she is." His voice sounded different, almost as if he was underwater.

I was nearly choking when I said, "Benny?"

"Well, it's not Emily Dickinson."

It was strange, as if his voice was coming from inside me. I looked around. It had to be some kind of joke. Or drugs. Maybe somebody had spiked the water fountain in the gym.

"Lindsay is a more difficult poet," he said. "His work is more complex, rhythmically and lyrically. It's harder for Jen to memorize. That's the problem. Plus, as everybody knows, Jen doesn't like to work on school things."

"I think she's working on a different poem," I said, as if it were normal to be chatting with him. My hands were shaking, but I was starting to feel warm inside. I checked him out more closely. He was wearing jeans and a sweatshirt. The lettering on his sweatshirt said: TIE GAME, and the words were shaped to form a tie. I remembered it as a joke Christmas present I gave him a few years ago.

"Nice shirt," I said. "The game never ends in a tie, though. There's always overtime."

"Tell me about it," he said.

The warm feelings took over completely. "I miss you," I said.

"Well, here I am."

I laughed. "You always wanted to know what went on in the girls' locker room, and here you are."

"Kind of boring."

My heart was bursting. Benny was here and we were having the talk I'd wished for. "Am I crazy?"

"Not crazy," he said. "Just Hemlock."

"It's not the Hemlock I know."

"It's the same old town, Brenda. You're changing, but Hemlock stays the same. It's like when you were young and Mom seemed so tall. Then one day she seemed short, but she didn't do anything. It was your body doing the changing."

"So I'm taller than Hemlock now?"

"Try not taking things so literally," he said.

"Oh, Benny. There's so much I want to talk to you about."

But he was distracted. He wrinkled his forehead and cocked his head.

"What is it?" I asked.

"Don't know exactly. Something's coming. Won't be long now."

"What won't be long?"

I glanced over to where he was looking but I didn't see anything. When I turned back, he was gone. And while my body seemed normal again, my mind wasn't. It raced with possibilities. Where had he come from? Where had he gone? Was I nuts?

I quickly got dressed and went outside.

It was dark. It's hard not to feel safe in a town as small as Hemlock, but tonight something didn't feel right. I'd stayed inside longer than I thought, and Jen was supposed to be my ride, but she'd left early. It was drizzling and I held my face up to feel the wet pinpricks. It's a cheap moisturizer. They can say what they want, but we girls who live in humid climates have it all over the desert girls when it comes to skin.

Mr. Hobbs's car was the only one left in the lot. He has a little car, a Morris Mini, but no one was in it. As I walked closer, I could see that his stuff was inside it. I opened the door and peeked in. His coat was thrown over the seat, and his notebook had spilled onto the mat below the wheel.

"Mr. Hobbs?" I called. "Mr. Hobbs?"

No answer. Maybe someone had come and picked him up. But wouldn't he have taken his things with him?

"Mr. Hobbs?"

I heard a squeak, like the sound of a new kitten. It squeaked again, lower this time. Given what had just happened in the locker room, I was a little nervous as I crept over to the edge of the parking lot. Beyond the cement was grass that sloped down to a group of ivy-covered trees. The cat sound was coming from the trees.

"Mr. Hobbs?" I tried once more.

I heard a garbled voice and saw an arm come out of the ivy. "Miss Dickinson?"

I jumped down the incline and ran over to him. He was all

bunched up like a porcupine protecting its belly. And he was missing his sweatpants. "Mr. Hobbs, what happened?"

He spit some ivy out of his mouth. "Methinks they got the best of me, dear Emily," he said.

"Who?" I asked.

"Don't really know. Can you help me up?"

I tried helping him stand, but he was too tangled in the ivy. In a small town you always expect someone will be there for you. But as I looked around, I knew this time I was going to have to be there for someone else.

"Hold on," I said to him, and then I ran back into the school and called my mom. When I got back to Mr. Hobbs, he was still trying to get up. "Can you stand at all?" I asked him.

"It does not look positive for that possibility," he said.

I sat down next to him and touched his shoulder. "Help is coming very soon," I said.

He twisted one hand out of the ivy and patted my shoe. "Miss Dickinson," he said, "I do believe you're coming around."

My mom came a few minutes later and I ran to meet her. She hugged me tightly. I think all this was reinforcing her idea that something bad was always lurking around the next corner. Then an ambulance screeched into the parking lot. My mom had called them, not knowing if Mr. Hobbs was hurt or not. They picked him up and put him on a stretcher, covering his lower half with a sheet. By that time quite a few people had shown up to watch, some of them still wearing bibs from dinner.

"I want to go with him," I whispered to my mom. She nodded, and we walked over to our car. The two of us followed the ambulance, its siren blaring, all the way to Chehalis.

The doctors took Mr. Hobbs right away, and Mom and I sat in the waiting room. "I don't like the looks of this," she said. She quizzed me about the whole incident. She asked me why I'd been all alone at school, but I sure wasn't going to tell her about seeing Benny. Instead, I said that Jen and I had lost track of time and I'd decided to walk home. She seemed satisfied with that.

After about fifteen minutes, Mrs. Hobbs came in. Mom shook her hand and they talked for a minute before Mrs. Hobbs went to see her husband.

"It looks like our work is done," Mom said. She stood up. But I wasn't ready to leave.

"I want to know that he's okay," I said.

My mother hesitated and then nodded. She sat back down, picked up a magazine, and started reading. I paced around the waiting room. It was empty except for Mom and me. I looked out the window and watched the night grow darker.

Finally, Mrs. Hobbs came out. "He'd like to see you, Brenda," she said.

I glanced at Mom, and she nodded. Mrs. Hobbs and I went in together.

Mr. Hobbs was lying in bed with his hands across his chest. His face lit up when he saw me. Even though they'd cleaned him up, I saw a faint swirl of dirt on his neck.

"Ah, Miss Dickinson," he said. "My heroine, my savior."

"Are you all right?" I asked.

"Fit as a fiddle," he quickly said. "Well, perhaps a fiddle in need of tuning. I hope this little incident hasn't harmed you in any way."

"Do you know who did this to you?"

"Not exactly," he replied. "And in the end it most likely doesn't matter."

"I think it does," I said. "People who do this kind of thing need to be punished."

"Perhaps they already feel punished, my dear. Life hasn't been easy lately in our little corner of the world."

I waited for him to say more, but he only rubbed at his neck. "I'm glad you're not badly hurt," I said. "I should be going, I guess."

"No," he said abruptly. "I want to tell you something. Goodness knows I could have some sort of cerebral setback from all the fuss, and I want you to know something just in case."

"Don't be dramatic," Mrs. Hobbs said from her chair in the corner.

"Ignore her," Mr. Hobbs said. "She's scared out of her wits, but she likes to cover her fears with sarcasm."

"What is it you want me to know?" I asked.

"Do you understand why I chose Miss Dickinson for you?"

I nodded. "Because you like her. She's one of your favorite poets."

"No, no," he said. "Or rather, yes, she is one of my favorites, but that's not the reason. I chose her because you remind me of her."

"I do?"

"Don't be coy," he said. "I'm sure you've read up on her, so tell me the salient features of her personality."

I ran through it in my head. Quiet. A recluse. Kept her work in a trunk. "I guess I don't see it," I said.

"Have you gotten to the part about refusing to present herself to the world? Her love affairs that bore fruit only through letters? Her living in the shadow and protection of her parents' home?"

"That reminds you of me?" I said.

"With a little poetic license, of course."

"But I don't think I'm a recluse," I protested. "I get out. I play basketball. I have friends."

"But what is your home, after all? Your house? Or is it the town you live in?"

I almost reminded him of going to other towns to away games, but I was beginning to see his point.

"If you recall, Miss Dickinson was more social and vibrant in her developing years. It wasn't until her twenties that she grew roots and never wandered farther than her own garden. My fear for you, Miss Dickinson, is that you will never go away to college, that you'll stay here to live the life you believe you were destined to live. I hate to think of all that promise, all that talent wasted."

"You chose Emily Dickinson for me . . ."

"So you could learn what you are not."

"And the others? Vachel Lindsay, Robert Frost?"

"The same reason."

I saw Mr. Hobbs for what he really was then. A teacher. A person who studied his students. Who wanted them to be more than they ever thought they could be. I leaned down and whispered in his ear. "I think you're not at all what everyone thinks you are."

"Thank you, Miss Dickinson," he said. "I think."

Then the nurse came in and told me I had to leave.

In the car on the way home, I stared out the windshield.

Mom tried to make small talk, but I only said "uh-huh" and "yeah."

At home I ran up to my bedroom and got out my book of poems. It was strange to think that our coach had spent so much time thinking about us not only as players but as people too. In the midst of all that was happening in our town, someone was actually paying attention to us.

I wanted to tell Benny all this. I had an odd feeling that if I tiptoed across the hall, I'd see him lying on his bed. It would be a constant comfort for me to have him by my side. I stood outside the door to his room for the longest time, wanting to see him and yet not. What would it mean if I turned out to be the girl who had a secret companion all her life? And that secret companion was her dead brother? I put my hand on the knob but then quickly drew it away. Maybe another time I would be more ready. Maybe then I would know what I really wanted to find inside.

# Chapter 11

The next day Mr. Hobbs's sweatpants were hanging at half-staff on the school flagpole. One of the boys stopped and saluted them on the way into school. In class everyone was talking about what had happened. There were lots of rumors floating around. Some people tried to blame a gang of teenagers, but there aren't any gangs in Hemlock. Others thought it was the work of a specific person who Mr. Hobbs had done wrong. Freddie blamed Napavine. But regardless of the explanation, almost everybody felt Mr. Hobbs had had it coming. Everybody but me.

You don't do that to a person, no matter what they've done. It's humiliating. It wasn't the physical bruises that bothered me as much as the bruises to his ego. You can make fun of Mr. Hobbs's stupid hat, but you shouldn't make fun of what made him want to wear it in the first place.

Practice was canceled that day to give him time to recuperate. I stayed around for a while after school, and that's when I saw Jen come out of the locker room with her gym bag.

"What are you doing?" I asked.

"Just getting the rest of my things," she replied.

"So you're going through with it," I said. "You're quitting?"

"That's right."

"Please don't," I said. "We need you."

She put her bag on the ground and kicked at it with her toe. "I can't do it, Bren. It's just too much. I talked to my mom and she agrees. I shouldn't have to do something that makes me feel bad."

"But maybe it will get better," I said. "You really need to talk to Mr. Hobbs. I know you'll see things differently if you just talk to him."

But she was shaking her head. "My mom came up with a good word for it," she said. "It's called dignity. She says a person can lose a lot of things in life, but you have to keep your dignity or no one will respect you. I don't feel one bit of dignity on the court anymore."

"It is embarrassing," I admitted. "So I can't talk you into staying?"

She shook her head. "I've got plenty of other things to do."

"I thought you wanted to play in college," I said.

"I do," she said. "I did." She put her head down, and I knew she was upset. When she looked back up, I could see tears in her eyes. "I don't know what I want."

"Jen?"

But she waved me away and picked up her bag. "See you," she said.

I called after her. "Jen, is it just Mr. Hobbs, or is it something else too?"

"What's that supposed to mean?"

"It means maybe there's something else going on besides basketball. Something that's got you down."

She shook her head. "Don't get all psych on me, Bren." She seemed ready to do one of her famous walk-offs, but she hesitated a moment. "It's just too hard. Wondering what's going to happen to this town. Wondering what my future is. I can't figure it out."

"I know it's easier just to let everything go on around us, Jen. But for now, what do we have if we don't have basketball?"

"You know, sometimes it's like you think you're Benny. All basketball, all the time. You Jacobsens have the corner on it. There's no room for the rest of us."

That hurt. I almost liked it better when she was apologizing for everything. "You know that's not true," I said.

She turned to go. "I just need time to think about it, Bren. It's all coming too fast."

It was true. Maybe none of us was prepared for all these changes.

"I just need a good reason," she said. "And nothing right now sounds like a good reason to keep playing."

"How about because you love the game?"

She looked wistful for a moment, as if she could see herself on the court. "I do love the game," she said. "But right about now it doesn't seem like the game loves me."

It was then I remembered my talk with Benny, when he said, "It's the same old town, Brenda. You're changing." I said, "The game does love you, Jen. Maybe we're just different people playing it."

She swung her bag up over her shoulder. "Maybe so. But I'm sick of different."

I watched her walk off. I knew exactly what she was going through, but there didn't seem to be anything I could say that would make her put on her uniform again. It was just like with my dad. If only there was a way to make people stop and think. To make my dad realize that I was still alive and needing him.

Just as Jen was about to turn the corner, I called out to her, "I'm going to change your mind!"

She turned briefly, then smiled and disappeared.

I didn't go home. Instead, I walked by the barbershop, but it was locked up tight. I kept replaying my talk with Benny in my head. When it came down to it, we hadn't really said much to each other. None of the good stuff, like what it's like in heaven, or what he does all day now. And besides the fact that I might have been going crazy, I felt good about it. Maybe Benny was still there for me and I wouldn't have to miss him so much anymore.

I'd just decided to head home when I heard a screech come from a street off Main/56. I recognized it immediately and started running toward the sound. I ducked in between the Fir Cone and the barbershop and ran onto the back street. There I saw what was making all the noise.

Mavis was in the front yard of her house, jumping up and down with her hands over her mouth. Every few seconds she pulled her hands away and let out a scream. It took me a second, but then I saw the reason for all the commotion. Right in the corner of the yard, near the street, someone had planted a fresh new FOR SALE sign.

I tried to give her a hug, but she pulled away and cried out again. "We're moving, Bren," she said. "Whether the house sells or not. We're going up to Olympia."

"Before the school year's over?"

"That's what Mom says. Dad got a job up there, and Mom says she can get one too." She looked ready to cut loose again, so I clamped my hand over her mouth.

"There's got to be something we can do," I said.

I called an emergency team meeting. I even left a message for Jen, but I didn't hear back from her. The rest of us met at Mavis's house, and we all tried to calm her down. When we asked her what she wanted to do, she said she wanted to go out to Fostoria. So we got into Freddie's car and drove to the lot. When we got there, Mavis jumped out and ran toward the mill. She scooped up a bunch of rocks and started throwing them at the main building.

She was screaming and cussing up a storm while the rest of us watched. That's when it hit me: This could happen to any one of us. Freddie and I locked eyes and I knew she was thinking the same thing. Pretty soon Mavis slumped to the ground, and I could hear her crying. Lena went over and held her.

"We can't let this happen," Freddie said.

"What are we going to do?" I asked.

"I don't know," Freddie answered. "But my mom says there's always something that can be done."

Lena and Mavis walked over to us then. Mavis had raccoon eyes from crying. "I think she killed the planer shed," Lena said.

Mavis laughed and dabbed at her eyes. Good old Lena.

Smart as a whip and she seemed to be getting a sense of humor. But she was upset too. I saw her wipe away her own tears when she turned her head.

"What can we do, Mavis?" I asked.

"Where's Jen?" she wailed. "Why isn't she here?"

I explained that I'd called her, but that wasn't good enough for Mavis.

"She has to be here," she said. "It isn't right that she's not."

"Should we go get her?" I asked Freddie.

"She won't come," Freddie said. "When I asked her about the team earlier, she told me to bite it."

"Well, maybe we should go to her," I said.

It was getting dark when Freddie pulled up to Jen's house. All four of us walked up to the porch together, and Mavis knocked on the door. When Jen's mom answered it, she looked surprised.

"I'm afraid she's shut up in her room," she said. "She may never come out again."

"Could you try?" Freddie asked.

But we didn't have to wait. From up above the porch came the sound of Jen's window opening. We all backed up onto the lawn.

"I'm not coming down," Jen warned. "So don't even try it."

"Get down here," Freddie demanded. "Don't even think that you can get rid of us that easy."

"Did you hear about Mavis?" I asked.

"I heard," Jen said.

"Well?" I asked.

"Well what?"

"She needs you."

Jen sat in her window for a while longer. The streetlight came on, casting its blue fluorescent light. It was getting colder, but still we all sat down on her front walk, hugging our knees. "Just a sec," Jen finally said. She came out a minute later with sweatshirts for all of us and sat down beside me.

"Listen," Freddie said. "Do you hear anything?"

"No," said Jen.

"Exactly what I mean," said Freddie. "Nothing. Nothing's happening in this town anymore."

"What do you expect?" Jen asked. "There's nothing here anymore."

"That's not true," I said. "We're still here. Doesn't that mean anything?"

"It does to me," Mavis said, sniffing.

"Me too," said Lena.

"I don't want to leave," Mavis said.

Lena reached over and rubbed her shoulder. "None of us wants you to go, either," said Lena.

"Is that true? Nobody does?" She peered over at Jen. "Is that true, Jen?"

"'Course it's true," Jen replied.

"Then don't you leave, either," Mavis said.

"I'm not."

"You're leaving the team," said Lena.

Jen opened her mouth to speak but then closed it. She picked up a piece of dead grass and twirled it in her fingers. "It's freezing out here," she finally said.

"Let's go then," I said.

"Where?" Freddie asked.

"You know where," I said. "I've got something important to tell you guys anyway."

We got up, but Jen took her time. I noticed she didn't put up much of a fight when I took her by the arm and pulled her over to Freddie's car. We all piled in and took a drive out to the town limits.

Freddie left the lights on so we could see the lettering on my grandpa's sign. We sat for a while, and then Jen said, "It looks different."

"That thing looks bigger every year," Freddie said.

"But everything else in town looks smaller," said Lena. "Remember the chairs in your dad's shop, Bren? Man, there was no way I could crawl into one of those ten years ago. Now it's easy as pie."

"Not that you'd ever want to get your hair cut there," Jen put in.

"Watch it," I said, but I liked that we were joking again.

"I'm sick of it," Freddie said. "I'm sick of that damn sign out here. Every time I look at the thing, it makes me want to puke. I'm sorry, Bren. I know it was your dad's team and all, but come on. How long do we have to look at it?"

"You don't have to tell me," I said. "That sign makes me sad."

"It makes me tired," said Mavis.

"I think Freddie's right," I said. "How long do we have to look at it?"

"Till somebody burns it down," Freddie said. "Or until some team in this town makes them have to change it."

"Exactly," I said with a smile.

"You know what would really be cool?" Freddie said, getting it. "To have them put a new sign up here. One that says 'State Champions' instead of that stupid 'Ninth Place.' And the best thing would be if *we* brought it home. Not the boys, like everybody expects. Kind of like the Napavine tree, only cooler. It would be worth it just for that."

"Worth what?" Jen asked her.

Freddie took a few seconds, but I knew she meant it. "Worth putting up with Mr. Hobbs and his dumb ideas."

"Well, speaking of Mr. Hobbs," I said. And I told them all about it. About finding him, about the ER, about our talk.

"Hold on," Jen said. "You mean, I remind him of Vachel Lindsay?"

"Maybe not in the way you think, but yes. His character, I think he means."

It was the perfect opportunity for Jen to say something snide, but she didn't. All she said was "Hmm."

It was quiet in the car for a while. I could feel the others spinning it around in their minds. "Just ask him to explain it," I finally said. "It'll make more sense coming from him."

We left soon after that and went back to Jen's. Then she gave me a ride back to my house. She was quiet most of the way, but when I opened the door to get out, she said, "Our parents could just up and leave too. Where would we be then?"

"Not here," I answered.

"Kind of makes you want to hang on."

"I wish you would come back to the team," I said.

"I'll think about it," she promised. Then she slapped the steering wheel with the palm of her hand. "It's more than Mr. Hobbs, Bren. It's more than basketball. I'm scared. Scared to leave. Scared to stay. I don't want to have to think about it."

"That's the bad part," I said. "But if you don't think about it, it won't get any better. The fact that you're thinking about it counts for something." I didn't know what else I could say, but I was hopeful when I got out of her car.

Upstairs in my room, I thought about everything. Jen was right. All the confusion in town made it hard. And like Mavis, any one of us might have to leave, whether we wanted to or not. Some things were out of our control. But there was one thing at least that we could do something about. Basketball.

I was glad we'd all gone out to the sign. It felt like we'd made a pact, and it gave me hope that we could become a team again. To represent Hemlock. To keep our dignity. To make a run for State. To play out who we were really meant to be.

Chapter 12

Eight of us showed up for practice the next day. We were all a little edgy, and Jen's not being in the locker room made it worse. I could see the disappointment in everyone's eyes. It's hard to keep a good feeling going when your hopes get dashed. And it didn't help much when we hit the gym floor and saw our coach bruised and limping.

We were pitiful the first ten minutes of practice. So pitiful that Mr. Hobbs called a break and sat us down in a semicircle around him.

"What is it, ladies?" he asked.

"Does it hurt?" Freddie asked.

Mr. Hobbs touched his neck. "No, Miss Millay, it doesn't."

"So you're still going to be our coach?" Lena asked.

Mr. Hobbs blinked his eyes hard. "What do you think? Am I going to let a little bend in the road get in the way of my goals?" He waited a moment and then answered his own question. "Absolutely not. Life is designed with pitfalls and periods of gracelessness. But it's also designed with moments of pure joy and determination. I am convinced that whoever did this to me was hoping I would quit as your coach. As you can see, that hasn't happened." He paused for effect and then asked, "What else can I clear up for you, ladies?"

None of us wanted to say anything. In fact, it was so quiet that we could hear every breath, every squeak of a shoe. So quiet that we all heard the door of the locker room open. I turned around and there was Jen, all dressed for practice. My first impulse was to run over and jump up and down like a gradeschooler, but I kept my cool. We all did.

She walked over to us and stood behind the circle. "I'm sorry, Mr. Hobbs," she said. "I'm sorry I quit the team. And I'm sorry someone did that to you." She looked down at us. "I'm sorry to you guys too. But if anybody says anything too mushy right now, I swear I'll go walking out the door again." She picked the ball up off the floor and bounced it, not looking at us.

"Apology accepted, Mr. Lindsay," Mr. Hobbs said. "Okay, girls, let's get back to the fray."

To work as a team you need a leader, and Jen was our leader. Right away she was herding the underclassmen around like a border collie. Even when Mavis tossed the ball and hit Jen in the side of the head, Jen just clapped her hands and shook it off. We did it again until we got it right, and it was like all our problems were gone for a while. Even Mavis's. Freddie had hatched a plan to have Mavis live with her family until the end of the year, and Mavis was bringing it up with her mom. On the court she played like a fire had been lit under her, like she had something new to prove. We all did, I guess.

Mr. Hobbs too. His limp didn't look too bad, and he assured us the bruises on his face would go away little by little. He took up right where he'd left off.

"You there, Miss Dickinson," he shouted at me. "Do you think you could find the courage to step out of the key once in a while? And Mr. Lindsay, a little less talk and a little more action, if you please." It was a test for Jen, but she just looked at me and put a smile on her lips.

We weren't perfect yet—far from it. Change takes time. We were still a little sloppy, but at least I wasn't the only one being passed the ball anymore. And the first time Jen got up to the line for foul-shot practice, she surprised us all.

"I've got my poem, Mr. Hobbs," she said.

The whistle fell out of Mr. Hobbs's mouth, but he quickly stuffed it back in.

Jen took aim at the basket and said:

> "No man should stand before the moon
> To make sweet song thereon,
> With dandified importance,
> His sense of humor gone."

She threw the ball up, and the only thing we heard was the swish of the net. Mr. Hobbs took the whistle out of his mouth and made like he was polishing it.

"Well?" said Jen.

"Not my favorite," Mr. Hobbs said. "But acceptable. Why that particular poem, Jennifer?"

She bounced the ball a few times and then stopped. "I don't know. It kind of jumped out at me. Like no one person is more than anything else. Like maybe we shouldn't think we're such a big deal. Full of ourselves or whatever."

We all stood around with our mouths hanging open. This was Jen, taking her poem seriously.

Mr. Hobbs smiled big and nodded his head.

It got even better after that. All the tension left the gym, and we started loosening up. We played with more confidence. We weren't so shy about our poems. Lena said "wings" loud and strong and forgot about the birds of night.

Things started changing at that practice and continued at the ones after. I didn't know if we were finally "in the zone," as Benny used to say, or if we were playing with a different part of our brain, the way Mr. Hobbs had talked about. But the gap between our play this year and last year was closing. I was able to focus better when I knew the rest of the team could too. Hemlock's problems faded for a while. There were even practices when I forgot about Benny. And a few weeks later, when Mavis's parents moved to Olympia, Mavis got to stay in town with Freddie and her family. We all were happy about that.

As much as we were changing, though, things at Fostoria weren't. Nobody talked about the mill reopening anytime soon. But having the mill closed wasn't a bad thing for girls' basketball. More fans showed up, because there was nothing else to do. And at the Adna game, something happened that made us think there might be a place for a strange team like ours in the world of girls' B basketball.

Nobody knew he was in the stands that Saturday night. Maybe someone had called him because of the Boistfort game or because my dad had gotten kicked out of all the league gyms. Whatever the reason, the high school sports editor from the biggest paper in Seattle came to the Adna game and sat a few rows behind our bench.

We were in fine form that night. Adna was a good team, but having the opposing squad recite poetry at the foul line threw normally good teams off guard. Mr. Hobbs's old hat hadn't been found, but he'd managed to stitch together an even better one, and he was a sight, limp-bouncing along the sidelines with a satin axe flopping on his head like a rooster's comb.

"Methinks she doth elbow too much!" he shouted to the ref while behind him, according to several loyal Lumberjack fans, the newsman patiently wrote his words down on a pad.

Of course the Adna fans took every chance to come up with their own poems. "Methinks thou is an idiot!" I heard over the roar of the crowd. I don't think the news guy bothered to write that down. But it was energizing even with all the trash talk—maybe because of it. It became easier to step up to the foul line, say my piece, and swish a couple of crucial points. One time, right before I started my poem, a kid from Adna yelled, "Because I could not stop for beer . . ." Even the ref smiled at that one.

Since the Boistfort game, the other girls had been true to their word: They weren't passing the ball just to me and making me the only one reciting at the line. It was still taking a while for some of them to relax, though. During Jen's first trip to the line, I saw her face getting redder than normal. And Mavis chewed on her lip and narrowed her eyes as she looked to the basket. Only Freddie seemed to love it all. Hands on her hips, she winked at the boys who threw catcalls her way.

She walked right up to the line and shouted out Edna St. Vincent Millay's words louder than she needed to:

> "My candle burns at both ends;
> It will not last the night;
> But ah, my foes, and oh, my friends,
> It gives a lovely light!"

We won the Adna game by thirteen.

The next day Mom called from the Interstate Quik-Mart and told me to get down there pronto. I thought I might ride my bike, but the rain gods had decided to pay a visit again, so I called Jen and got her out of bed to drive me.

Jen grabbed two maple bars while Mom handed me the Seattle paper. If my mom had been a cat, she would have already swallowed the canary.

"Section B, page seven," she blurted out.

Jen chewed and looked over my shoulder. There it was, section B, page seven: a small picture of an Adna girl and me fighting for the ball right next to an article called "Poetry in Motion."

I couldn't help glowing. Even Benny's picture had never been in a paper this big. Here I was, just a high school girl from a small town in southwest Washington with my picture on the very same page as professional basketball players. And the article was great too, like a Sunday-night newsmagazine show, featuring a human interest story in a small town. The reporter wrote about our team like we were special, like we were a miracle from deep in the woods.

"Cool," Jen said. "But where's my picture?"

"Come on," I complained. "You got a whole paragraph. What more do you want?"

"Easy for you to say. You're a star."

I looked at the picture more closely. It didn't really look like me. My face was contorted and my eyes were half closed. I was fighting hard for the ball, but the Adna girl had her elbow in my side. It was weird seeing myself in that pose. I looked almost like my dad. I'd seen him so many times out on the court, focused and struggling to get the ball. Like nothing was going to get in his way. Nothing was getting in my way, either, from the looks of this photo.

I bought a couple more papers and went back home. When I got there, the phone was already ringing off the hook. Jen and I took turns answering calls from well-wishers. It seemed like hours passed. Our voices got hoarse, but we didn't complain. The best call came after Jen left: It was long distance from Ms. Cochran.

"What's going on up there?" she asked. "Has that town lost it?"

I brought her up to date, and I could hear her clicking her tongue all the way through my story.

"Do you want me to talk to Mr. Hobbs?" she asked. "Maybe I can set him straight."

"But we won," I said. "And we were good."

"Well, the reason is plain and simple talent," she said. "You girls are excellent ball players." I asked about her team, and she said they were in a building year. "What we need is an infusion of raw talent," she said. "Do you know of anybody?"

The idea just popped into my head. "Maybe I should go there," I said.

There was a long pause on the other end and then Ms. Cochran laughed. "I don't mean major talent like you, Brenda. Just some good raw coachable talent. You, young lady, are destined for bigger things."

"Do you really think so?"

"Don't play innocent, Brenda. We've been through this before. Have you applied to any of the schools we talked about last year?"

"Yes."

"To Oregon?"

"Yes. And Mr. Hobbs has been pushing me about the University of Washington."

"Good," she said. "Very good. You know, I'm going to talk to a couple of coaches I know down here. See what they can come up with."

"Thanks, Ms. Cochran," I said. We talked for a few more minutes, and then she had to go. Before saying goodbye, I heard her mutter under her breath, "Poetry, my eye."

After I hung up, I thought about my dad. An idea had been dogging me since I first saw my picture in the paper, so I put on my jacket and headed out.

The door to the Jacobsen Barber Emporium was open, so there was no bell to announce my arrival. Hair littered the floor, and my dad's combs and razors could have used a good washing. It looked like the haircuts for his friends that day had done a good business. I heard the TV going in the back, so I peeked in.

Dad was sitting on the couch in his robe, chewing on a piece of pizza. The place smelled like cigarettes and stale beer, and a pro game was on TV.

"Hello?" I said, stepping in.

"Who's there?" he said, not bothering even to look.

"Me. I brought you something." I had to fight the feeling that I might not be welcome. "Have you seen this?" I handed him the article.

He looked it over. "I'll be damned," he said.

"It's a funny picture."

He looked at it again. "I think it's hard to look good when you're fighting for the ball." He started to hand it back.

"No, you can keep it," I said.

"Okay." He laid it down on top of the pizza box. "So, how's it going?"

"You know. Okay." When you live with people, it's always easier to get in the rhythm of talking to them. I was definitely out of rhythm with my dad. "I wish you could have been there," I said.

"Yeah, well, you know how that goes. The jerks from the league want to keep a guy from watching his own daughter."

"Maybe they could make an exception," I tried.

"Maybe," he said. "But doubtful. This world's punishing your old man."

"Dad?" I said. "How are you and Mom doing?"

He fidgeted, and I knew I'd asked the wrong question again. It had been going so well. Why did I have to go and screw it up?

"You don't have to answer if you don't want to," I added.

He shrugged and picked up the pizza again. "It'll all work out. It always does."

I couldn't remember any other time when their marriage was in trouble. As far as I could tell, their fights before had been just like the ones other married couples around town had. Nothing big. Nothing like what was happening now.

"Your mom will come to her senses," he said.

I walked over and sat down in a chair. "What's the matter, Dad?"

He stopped eating and looked at me. "With your mom and me? We're just having a disagreement right now. It's nothing you should be worrying about."

"But I am worried," I said.

"Well, don't be."

And that should have been it. It was clear he didn't want to talk about it anymore. Maybe it was the game the night before or maybe even my talk with Benny, but I didn't want to leave it that way. So I broke one of the rules.

"Is it Benny, Dad?" I asked.

He squinted his eyes. "What?"

"Are you thinking more about Benny now that basketball's here? I know I am."

"Brenda." I felt the warning.

"I was just wondering."

He took a long time to answer. He played with the edge of his robe and moved the ashtray farther away. "You don't understand, Brenda. And what good's talking about it? It doesn't change the fact that your brother's gone. So let's just not bring it up, okay?"

I nodded. I waited another minute, but this time he really was done talking, so I said goodbye and left.

On the way home I felt my anger take over. Here I was a senior in high school and he still wanted to talk to me like I was ten. I hated the way he'd cut me off. I wanted to talk about Benny with him. I wanted to talk about Benny with my mom. He was my brother, after all.

I felt nervous and jumpy, and I knew there was really only one way for me to get rid of that feeling. I ran the rest of the way home to find my ball.

# Chapter 13

It had started to rain, but I went out to the playground anyway and shot around. I wasn't just mad at my parents. I was angry at myself too. Maybe Dad talked to me like I was ten because sometimes I acted like it. What did I think? That I could cure whatever was going wrong with his and Mom's marriage?

But on the other hand, I knew I deserved the right to talk about Benny. He was my brother. My coach. My confidant. It wasn't fair for me to be shut out. I gritted my teeth and bounced the ball on the wet court.

Rain always feels good to me. It seeps into my skin like a natural drug, calming me, fortifying me, balancing me. After a while I stopped noticing the splashes the ball made. The rain turned warm and felt like thousands of tiny kisses.

I was concentrating so hard on my shooting, I didn't notice that a few people had stopped by the playground to watch. It was only when I made a tough fadeaway fifteen footer that I heard applause. I turned around and there were Jen's mom, wearing her plastic rain hat, and Officer Parsons, the deputy sheriff, with his car window rolled down and his elbow hanging out. They both waved at the same time. I waved back and kept on shooting. The next time I turned around, there were three more people braving the weather and watching.

I'm not much for being the center of attention, so I was glad when Jen came running down the street, slipping on her windbreaker as she did.

"What's going on?" she asked, noticing the crowd.

"I don't know. Your mom started it." We both looked over and Jen's mother waved again.

"The real question is, What are you doing out here?" she said.

"It's a long story. Here, break for the basket." She did, and I lobbed the ball just in time for her to lay it up against the backboard.

We played around like that for a couple of minutes, and then I saw Mavis and Freddie walking toward us from the other side of the court. Freddie's mom had parked next to Jen's and they were talking.

Lena's dad drove up and let her out before settling in his seat to read a book.

"I'm glad you all decided to show up," Jen said. "It looks like Miss Dickinson here has been trying to hold a practice without us."

I tossed the ball at her, but she was too quick and caught it.

More cars started arriving. In Hemlock you don't need phone lines or the Internet or TV to get your news. It just happens. I could stop to cough by Maida's Drugstore, and by the time I got to the end of the street, someone's mother would be there with a spoonful of cough syrup, telling me to get to bed. So if someone is shooting baskets at the playground, before you know it, a crowd will probably be there.

Soon the older guys started showing up with that pickup game look in their eyes. This sport never gets out of their blood. And it wasn't long before I saw my dad get out of the Schultzes' car and stretch. All the guys followed him onto the playground. I think they were surprised that we were still there. For a moment it was like one of those Wild West showdowns: The older guys stood in a group on one side, and the starters on the girls' team were on the other. It was the old generation facing down the new. When we girls were younger, we would have tossed the ball in their direction and run screaming off the court. But now it was different. For some reason our feet stayed planted.

"Come on, girls," my dad said. "We're going to have a game."

Jen surprised us all by saying, "We'll be done in a sec."

My dad and the other guys looked thrown. The Schultz twins wrinkled up their foreheads as if Jen was speaking a different language.

"Uh, maybe we should take off," I whispered.

"Why?" Jen said. She took a step forward and puffed up her chest. "We have just as much right to be here as they do." From behind, I could see that one of her hands was shaking.

"But you know the rule," I whispered.

She turned and stared at me like I was a traitor. "What rule?" she said. Then she turned back. "Show me where it's written that we don't get to use this court just as much as anybody else."

Hearing that, I did start to feel like a traitor. Of course there was no rule. No written one. And here I was just ready to walk off and let myself be intimidated by nothing more than a tradition.

"Brenda?" my dad said in that voice of his that lets you know he means business. "We're going to need the court."

On the other side of the court I saw the parents start to take notice. Jen's mom and Freddie's mom had stopped talking. Even Lena's dad had gotten out of his car. I didn't know what to say. My heart was telling me it wasn't right what the men were trying to do, but my brain told me we didn't stand a chance against them. The confusion froze my feet. No matter how hard I tried, they wouldn't budge. I needed to have a serious discussion with my body about the way it was starting to do things on its own.

From the corner of my eye I saw my mom's car pull up.

My dad walked toward me and stopped a few yards away. "Brenda?" he said. "What are you doing?"

"We're shooting around," I said.

"I can see that. But come on. What are you doing? We need the court."

"And when they're finished, you can have it."

This time it wasn't Jen or me. It came from my mom. She walked over to our side of the court. "Can't you guys be a little polite once in a while?" But before they could answer, she added, "In case you haven't noticed, these girls have won their last three games. And they want to practice, so they can win some more."

"Give me a break," my dad said.

My mom's eyes made slits. "No more breaks," she said flatly. "All the time it's you, you, you. And that goes for all of you guys. Sure, you're out of jobs and that hurts. But do you think

123

it affects only you? Do you think the rest of us are just taking it all in stride? You're not the only ones living here and having to put up with what's happened. We're all suffering."

This would sound good if you were watching it on a TV show, but these were my own parents airing their dirty laundry.

"Leave them alone!" Jen's mom shouted. She and Freddie's mom were coming out on the court. "They were here first. Let them play."

Lena's dad came out too and leaned against the fence. "Look, Bren," Dad said, ignoring the others. "We're getting a game together. I don't know what the hell's going on here, but we need the court. You can go get behind the fence and watch."

"No," Jen said. "We don't want to go behind the fence."

"We're tired of being behind the fence," Lena added.

"And they shouldn't have to be," Mom said. "These girls are a class act. Practically the only ones left in this town. So why are you treating them this way? You guys should be ashamed of yourselves "

And there was something shameful about the way they looked. Middle-aged guys with their bellies stretched out of shape, the rain wetting their hair and dripping down their faces. These were our fathers, uncles, cousins, brothers. I felt sorry for them. And maybe after everything that had happened with the mill, they did deserve to have the court to themselves and to have a good time for a change. But my feet still wouldn't move.

The rain pelted us all. I had to rub the back of my arm across my eyes so I could get a good look at my dad. He was just standing there, granite faced. A monument to the past in-

stead of the present. The tension rose and fought the relent-
less downpour. Then suddenly they started to leave. The
Schultz twins went first, bolting for their car. Then a couple of
other guys followed them off the court. Jen's and Freddie's
moms and Lena's dad went back to their cars. But there we
were: the girls' team and my dad, staring each other down.
The greatest living basketball player ever to hit the courts of
Hemlock against a gaggle of old wet poets.

It seemed like five minutes, but really it was probably just a
couple. Eventually, my dad shook the water off his head, and
it twirled around him like a halo. "This isn't the way it's supposed to work," he said. It was as if he'd just realized that
everyone—maybe everything—he'd ever loved was gone. He
gave me one last hard look and then took off.

I finally unstuck my feet from the court and took a step
toward him. "Dad!" I yelled.

He stopped and turned. Rain was running down his face,
and he spit it out in a spray. "You know, Brenda, your brother
would never have done anything like this. Never."

It was as if I had needles in my tongue and I couldn't get
out what I wanted to say. I felt the words form in my brain.
"No, Dad, Benny might have done something like this." But
they wouldn't come out. Would I ever be able to say to him
what was on my mind?

Mavis walked up alongside me. "Uh-oh," she said.

"What just happened?" Freddie asked.

Jen turned and smiled. "I think we just won the whole
thing."

But I knew that when you win one thing, you sometimes
lose another.

Chapter 14

Winning changes things. Where once we were just the opening act for the boys, now we were getting plenty of attention of our own. No one could remember the boys even being mentioned in the Seattle papers, so we finally had one up on them. And the boys' team continued to be mediocre, so their fans started gravitating toward us. We still got teased a lot. Some of the younger, goofier kids repeated the things they'd heard at the game, like "Because I could not stop for beer . . ." But even I was beginning to think it was a pretty funny joke.

Practices got even better. It felt like we'd always had Mr. Hobbs as our coach and his unconscious strategy did seem to work. We fell into a rhythm without even thinking about it. Instead of pulling us apart, the poetry began drawing us together. I liked hearing Lena go on about the wings of night, and when Jen said the word "dandified," it always cracked me up. Freddie just loved talking about her and Edna burning the candle at both ends. Mavis was great at helping us laugh at ourselves.

"Come on, Mr. Frost," she'd say. "Which road should I choose? Quick, before the ref blows his whistle. The one less traveled by? But why that one?"

"You can't end a sentence with a preposition," Lena would say. "You mean 'by the one less traveled.' And no, you shouldn't choose that one, because you'll get lost."

They calmed me, those practices. They helped me get through December.

After the standoff on the playground, my parents talked to each other even less. I was able to focus on basketball, but whenever I saw my mother sitting in the stands alone, I was reminded that my parents no longer lived together. And I always wondered where my dad was on game nights. It took a lot of three-point shots to get that out of my head.

There was also still Benny to think about. I'd come up with a system, so that whenever I thought of him and felt that funny vibration in my body, I would visualize myself pushing Benny into my heart and locking him in with a little key. Doing that seemed to keep things under control, so as the days went by, my fears about going nuts began to fade. This isn't bad, I said to myself. I can do this.

By now our team's fame was spreading. We'd been on a winning streak since the Adna game, so everyone wanted a look at us. The stands were packed wherever we played, and we had special cheering sections reserved just for Hemlock fans that were filled with people we didn't even know. Who would have thought that poetry could make such an impact on the Western Lewis County League?

While earlier in the season fans from opposing teams had mimicked us and been sarcastic, now our supporters drowned them out with selections from their own favorite poets. Anything from Theodore Roethke to a pornographic limerick, from Elizabeth Barrett Browning to a wicked variation on "Roses Are Red." By rights, all should have been well.

But the novelty of rhyme had gone away for our opposing teams. This was especially true for the Mossyrock girls one night in January. Instead of being distracted and frustrated, they were just mad. And when you're mad, you tend to foul. For some reason they liked to foul me.

So sometime in the fourth quarter, with our team up by a comfortable twenty-one points, I found myself at the foul line. I could hear the anticipation in the stands, as the fans were about to recite with me. I ignored them, said my poem, and sank the first shot. It was when I was bouncing the ball for my second shot that the world pulled itself out from under me.

*"Because I could not stop for Death"*—bounce-bounce—*"He kindly stopped for . . ."*

I froze. I could still hear the echo of the ball bouncing on the court, as if it was trailing off in the distance. But when I looked down, I had it securely in my hands. As the echo faded, it seemed like someone ran past me so fast that he sucked the air right out of my lungs. I couldn't catch my breath. For an instant I thought that I might die right there on the court. My heart took off racing, but I was standing stock-still.

Jen was lined up waiting for the rebound. I tried to say something to her, but nothing came out. My lips opened and closed without a sound. I looked up into the stands for my mom and then over to the bench where Mr. Hobbs had his arms out, palms up. That was the last thing I saw. Spots floated in front of my eyes and then it all went black. I felt myself fall to the court.

Whistles blew, feet trampled on the bleachers, and voices buzzed around me like bees. But it all faded slowly, like the end of a sad song. The last thing I heard was Jen saying, "What are we going to do now?"

Mom was sitting in a chair next to the hospital bed when I woke up. I vaguely remembered her riding in the back of an ambulance with me, but I had faded in and out. Dad was standing by the window. What was left of his hair stood straight up on his head, and I could see why. He kept rubbing it back and forth like a nervous kid.

"Oh, thank God," Mom said when I opened my eyes. She leaned over me and grabbed one of my hands. There was an IV snaking out of my arm.

"What happened?" I asked.

Dad came over and stood at the foot of the bed. "You okay, kid?"

I tried to move my head, but it hurt.

"You passed out," Mom said. "You hit your head pretty hard on the floor."

"Did we win?" I asked.

"Yes," she said softly. "How do you feel?"

"Like I don't know what happened. Is something wrong with me?"

"They're going to do tests, sweetie," Mom said. Her lip trembled.

"What kind of tests?"

"Now, don't get her all hepped up," Dad said. He rubbed his head again. "There's no use for it. The kid's as healthy as a horse."

But I could tell he didn't believe what he was saying. He was clamping his teeth together, the way he does when things aren't going right.

"Am I going to die?" I asked.

"See?" My dad again. "See what you've done?"

"Of course you're not going to die, Bren. The doctor thinks maybe it was an attack of nerves. They're just doing some tests to be sure."

"But they already gave me tests the last time," I wailed.

"It's not nerves," Dad pronounced. "There's no Jacobsen who goes down because of nerves. I say we get a second opinion."

Mom turned to him. "I think you should keep your opinions to yourself."

And they probably would have gone on like that if the nurse hadn't come into the room and shooed them out. Dad left in a hurry, but Mom doesn't like to be shooed, so it took her a few minutes. Eventually, it was just the nurse and me.

She busied herself around the room, straightening my pillows and checking my water bottle. "Your head's going to hurt for a while," she said. "But the doc says you don't have a concussion."

"What tests are they going to do?"

"Tests?" she said. "Oh, don't you worry yourself about that. If they *don't* do tests, that's when you should worry." I waited for her to go on, but she said she had to get something and left the room.

So what did that mean? Was she afraid to tell me I had

only hours to live? When she came back in, she brought me a pill.

"It'll help you sleep," she said. There must have been something strong in that pill, because it did a lot more than just put me to sleep.

I saw Benny again that night. He was standing right at the foot of my bed, where Dad had been earlier, and he had on a suit, like the one he wore when he made the All Western Lewis County League team as a sophomore. His hair was clipped too short, and part of it fanned up in the back like tiny hemlock seedlings. It made me laugh.

"What?" he asked.

"Your hair."

He reached up and rubbed at it, just like Dad had done. "Don't ever go to the Jacobsen Barber Emporium," he said.

"It happened again," I said. "This time I fainted at the foul line."

"I know."

"You weren't there. How do you know about it?"

He shrugged and kind of half smiled. "I know everything that happens to you."

"I guess you heard about Mom and Dad."

"It must be tough on you. How are you holding up?"

"I have basketball."

He tipped his head back, looking at the ceiling. "Basketball. Now, there's a game I could sink my teeth into again."

"I'd love to see you play just one more time."

He smiled and raised a bushy eyebrow at me. "I'm afraid that's not in the cards."

"It seems so unfair, Benny." I felt my heart constrict and wanted to cry. But I held it in.

"I don't make the rules, Bren," he said. "I just have to live by them. Or die by them, I guess."

"It bothers me that I don't know why you're here. Don't get me wrong—I love seeing you—but I just don't get it."

"It's simple. I'm here for you."

"Not for Mom or Dad?"

"No, just you."

"It's because I'm crazy, isn't it? It's because I'm going to die and you're here to lead the way to wherever it is you are."

He pressed his lips together into his serious look. "I think you're making this bigger than it actually is."

"I'm lonely, Benny. I have all my friends around, I go to school and pass people in the halls, but the whole time I feel like I'm all by myself."

"Do something about it, then. Talk to people. Open up."

"Who could I open up to?"

"You talked to Darwin, didn't you?"

"But Darwin's not going to make the loneliness go away. I think he understands, but he's not somebody I can talk to whenever I want."

"Who, then? Who would understand?"

Mentally I went through the list of people I knew and rejected them all.

"What about Jen?" he asked.

"No," I quickly said. "Not any of the girls on the team. They already think I should be in the nut house."

He sighed. "I guess Mr. Hobbs is right. You are Emily Dickinson."

"Don't you start," I warned.

"You should hear yourself. Saying 'yes, but' to every suggestion. You want to be lonely."

"I do not. It's just too hard."

"Nothing's too hard, Brenda. There's always a way to figure life out. You know, just play the game."

"You mean, basketball?"

"Whatever it is. You're good at basketball. You can figure out things on the court. Pretend your life is like being on the court. It'll come to you."

"But can I do this?"

"Give it up, Brenda," he said sharply.

"Give up what?"

"Give up being the one hiding in the shadows. I know you can find a way. You think I don't see you sneaking into my room and taking my socks out of the closet?"

"They bring me luck."

"Whatever they bring you, the point is you found a way to deal with it. You forgot about asking Dad, didn't you? You just went right in there and took the socks for yourself."

He was right. I had done that. I smiled at the thought.

"And the way you guys stood your ground out there on the elementary school court."

"But I couldn't say what I wanted to say."

"You will. You get more than one chance, you know."

"I was right, though, wasn't I?" I said. "You would have stood up to them."

"I love that you know things about me that Mom and Dad would never know."

It was odd. Like Benny and I knew each other better now than when he was alive.

"You're a great person, Brenda," he said. "You're a great basketball player. Act like it."

And then, suddenly, someone pulled the water plug and I

started crying. I couldn't control myself. I turned over and buried my face in the pillow. Nothing physical was hurting anymore, but inside was a whole lot of pain. Crying seemed to purify me. It flushed all the bad feelings out for the time being. And by the time it let up and I was only sniffling, Benny was gone.

# Chapter 15

The next day they released me from the hospital. My head still hurt, but I was told it would go away. The doctor had wanted to give me a referral to a therapist, but I talked him out of it. He wouldn't budge, though, about not allowing me to practice for a few days. And he said I shouldn't play any more games until I was feeling better.

I waited for Mom to tell him he didn't know what he was talking about, but she just nodded her head. All the way home I wondered what my life would be like without basketball.

At school I tried to avoid talking about what had happened, but everyone wanted to know what it was like to pass out in front of all those fans. I told them I'd had an allergic reaction to some medicine, but when they asked what kind of medicine, the only thing I could think of was allergy medicine. So instead of calling me Emily, they all got a kick out of calling me Al.

I definitely did not want to go talk to a counselor. Mom was nudging me to do it, but I stood my ground. I know what it means in this town to go see one. If anyone says the name Darwin Ostrander, we all think of the mental hospital.

But I sure wished I knew what was going on with me. I went to the gym and watched the team practice. No one understood why I couldn't be down there on the court with them. I looked healthy enough. I laughed with the kids at school and did my homework and took quizzes. Why shouldn't I be able to practice?

A few nights later there was another rumor about the tree, so I went down to City Hall. A lot of kids from school turned out, and a few adults were there too. Most of the men were standing in a group next to the tree. Only Darwin Ostrander was sitting on a rock off by himself. Once in a while one of the men would go across the street to the Fir Cone, and a few minutes later a different one would come out and take his place by the tree.

I hung around with the girls' team. Lena had a clipboard out and was working on her homework. Jen was trying to distract her, but Lena was having none of it.

"This is boring," Jen said, finally giving up on Lena and coming over to me. "Isn't there something better to do?"

"Like what?" I asked.

"Anything is better than this."

"Who starts these rumors, anyway?" Freddie asked.

"I think our parents do," Jen said. "It keeps us off the streets."

"Some streets," said Mavis.

Jen was right; it was boring. Not that saving the tree wasn't important, but it seemed like there might be better things to think about now. I sat down on a rock not far from where Darwin was. Just before our shift was over, I saw him get up and walk across the street. I thought he was going inside the Fir Cone, but the Schultzes came staggering out instead and Darwin just kept walking. I looked over at the girls, and they were still busy gossiping, so I got up and headed across the street.

"Darwin!" I called.

He turned around just as Stan Schultz grabbed for my arm. "Brenda, Brenda, Brenda," he said, his words slurring. "Recite me some of that poetry." I jerked my arm back.

"Come on," Stew said, pulling on his brother. "You've got to go home and sleep it off."

"But she wants to, don't you, Brenda?" Stan said.

"That's it!" Darwin yelled. He came stomping up and grabbed Stan by the collar. Stew just stepped aside and watched as Darwin dragged Stan over to their car and stuffed him inside. "You better take him home," Darwin said to Stew.

Stew got in and started up the car. He hung his head out the window. "Sorry, Brenda," he said. Then he peeled out.

Darwin came over to me. "You okay?"

"Yeah. But what's the deal with them?"

"The usual. They're just drunks."

I nodded toward the Fir Cone. "Think my dad was in there with them?"

"I haven't seen him. You going to be okay?"

I looked Darwin straight in the eye then. He seemed so serious, as if he knew what I was thinking. "Could I ask you something, Darwin?"

"Sure," he shrugged. "Shoot."

"Can we walk?"

Darwin stuffed his hands into his pockets as we took off down Main/56. His sneakers crunched in the gravel at the side of the road. Right around Maida's, I said, "I know people have made fun of you, Darwin, ever since your wife died and you had to go away." I paused to see how he was taking that.

"What is it you want to ask, Brenda?"

"I don't know quite how to say it, so here goes. I've seen Benny a couple of times. But not really. I mean, sometimes I think I see him."

As soon as it was out, I worried I'd said the wrong thing. But Darwin stopped and kicked at the gravel. "Do you think I'm crazy, Brenda?"

"What? No. I don't think that."

"Then why tell me about seeing your brother?"

"I don't know. I guess I thought maybe you would understand."

He shook his head and looked back up the street. The tree was all lit up by the streetlight and surrounded by townspeople. "Come on," Darwin said. He took me by the arm, and we went into an alley behind Maida's. It was darker there, and I stepped right into a big mud puddle. I hopped out and shook my foot.

"Be careful," Darwin said.

"Where are we going?"

"Away from ears."

We walked past the Petersons' garage and down their driveway to the street. I could see the sign in Mavis's front yard. Up and down the street, lights shone out of living room windows.

"Well, you haven't asked me the question yet," Darwin said, "but I know what it's going to be. So here's how it is. You can ask me this one time, and then I don't want to talk about it again. Is that a deal?"

I nodded. "Deal."

He leaned closer. "I see Margie all the time."

"All the time?"

"Pretty much."

"Doesn't it scare you?"

He laughed. "Why should it? I want to see her. Don't you want to see Benny?"

I didn't know how to answer that. "Do you worry that people will think you're nuts?"

"They already think that. And anyway, I don't care. When have you seen him?"

I told him about both times. We walked along the street as I talked. The funny thing was, I didn't care if anyone heard me. Finally, we stopped under a streetlight about a block away from the other side of Mavis's. I expected Darwin to ask me something else, but he just stood there staring at me.

I couldn't wait any longer. "Do you think I'm losing my mind, Darwin? Besides the fact that I see my dead brother, I'm fainting on the basketball court, going to the hospital. And they never find anything wrong with me. That all points to crazy as far as I'm concerned."

He grinned and snorted. "You know what I learned through all this? Who knows what normal is? Who knows what crazy is? Look around you. The only livelihood this town has ever known has been shut down, and a lot of the people here are going around pretending the damn thing's still operating.

They're making plans for their summer vacations and still want to remodel their houses. Does that seem sane to you? So whether it means anything to you or not, my answer to your question is, No, you're not crazy."

"Then what's going on with me?"

"Hey, I'm no shrink. If I was, maybe I wouldn't have the problems I do."

"It's so weird, Darwin."

"Welcome to my world," he said.

"Everything's different."

"Listen, Brenda. Margie told me something once. I mean, when she was alive. She said, 'There's no use harping on the way things are. It's just life. And the only thing you can be sure of in life is that things will change.' So if things seem all different to you, it's because that's the way life works."

It must have taken me too long to respond, because Darwin scuffed his shoes on the pavement and said, "I think I'll get going." He stuffed his hands into his pockets again and took off down the street, disappearing when he stepped into the streetlight's shadow.

I couldn't help but think how strange a conversation we'd just had. Imagine talking right out in the open about seeing dead people. But I knew Darwin wouldn't tell anybody. It would only come back on him if he did.

I headed for home. The rest of them would have to guard the tree. All the way down the street, I tried to remember exactly what Benny had said when I'd seen him. Most of it was true. I did stand in his shadow. But it had always seemed right. He was the star, and that's what happens when you have an older brother. Only now there was no older brother to tell me what to do. What happens when you step out of the shadow? You can figure it out, Benny had said. I know you can do it.

Maybe I could.

"You will go to practice tomorrow," I said out loud in my driveway. And I felt better just saying it. So what if I had confided in a guy everybody thought was crazy? Maybe the truth was that he wasn't crazy. Maybe he just thought about things in a different way. And maybe that's what I needed to do too.

Chapter 16

I went to the next practice and started at the next game. At first I felt self-conscious, but I sank both shots on my first trip to the foul line, and it was smooth sailing from there. Benny was right. I could do this. We beat Morton, 71–49, and we had incredible team harmony during the whole game. Or, as Mr. Hobbs told us afterward, "You ladies gave a whole new meaning to poetic justice."

After the boys' game, Mr. Hobbs put his arm on my shoulder and walked me out of the gym. "How you feeling, my dear?" he asked.

"I'm good," I said.

"We've won thirteen in a row. The Tacoma paper came out this morning and has us ranked fifth. That's considerably higher than we would have hoped. Did you see the stands tonight? Completely full. They're watching you, Emily. Are you going to be okay?"

"Maybe they're just watching to see if I'll pass out again."

"I hardly think so," he said. "They're not ghouls."

"I'm really fine," I said. "I think I was just overtired. I'm better now. Really."

"Your play on the court tonight would attest to that, I think."

Out in the parking lot people walking by patted my back and told me I'd done well. Mom was hurrying to the Quik-Mart, and I didn't know where Jen was, so I started walking home. About halfway down the street I saw Eric leaning against his car. "That was an awesome game you guys played," he said. His hair was glistening from the shower he'd taken.

"You think so? I thought I was a little slow."

"No, I was a little slow," he said. "You can't get much slower than riding the pine."

"Quit feeling sorry for yourself," I told him. "You're better than that."

"Yes, ma'am," he said, and saluted me. He reached down and scooped up a handful of gravel and started bouncing pieces into the street.

"Give me some of that," I said.

As he poured half of it into my palm, I could feel the heat from his hand when it brushed against mine.

"Now, how do you do this?" I asked.

"Well, try not to hit anyone when you bounce them in the street. People tend to get offended by that."

I threw one out, and it died before it had a chance to bounce. "This may not be my best sport," I said.

"Watch this," he said. He intentionally threw one toward a kid who was running behind his parents. It skipped against his leg, and he stopped to look around.

I giggled, although I've never been much of a giggler. I took my turn, with the same disappointing results. "Still looking to get out of town, Eric?" I asked him.

"Sure. You?"

"Thinking about it. Will you ever come back?"

"No." He stopped in midthrow. "Hmm."

"What's the 'hmm' about?"

"I guess I've never said that out loud before." He pointed to his chest. "Kind of gets you right here."

"I heard you got early acceptance," I said.

"Yeah," he said. "To Bates." He saw the questioning look on my face. "It's a small school in Maine. A lot of guys in the family have gone there."

"You and I are so different, Eric. No one in my family has gone to college yet. Benny was going to be the first."

"You get good grades. You're a star in basketball. You should have applied to some places back east. They like recruiting students from the west."

I shook my head. "I don't think that's for me."

"Could be," he said. "Even in my family, somebody had to be the first to go."

"God, it's hard enough just thinking about leaving Hemlock, much less going that far away."

He was pensive then; he kept grinding the gravel in his hand.

"Your skin's going to be a mess if you keep doing that," I finally told him.

He cupped his hand and let the gravel filter out like sand. "You want a ride home?" he asked.

"I can walk," I said.

"I know you can walk," he said. "But it's on my way."

"All right," I said. "Sure."

I got in and we pulled onto the street. The inside of his car was as spotless as the outside and smelled like pine cleaner. It took only a couple of minutes to get to my house. He parked in my driveway and then held on to the wheel like we were going a hundred miles an hour.

"Well," I said, "thanks for the ride."

"You too," he said. "I mean, you're welcome."

We sat there a minute not saying anything. It was uncomfortable, but I didn't mind it. I finally opened the door and got out, and I watched as he drove away.

"This is good," I said. And it wasn't until I'd reached my back porch that I realized my house wasn't at all on his way home.

Our team was on a tear. We won another five in a row, and things were going like clockwork. Winning became an expectation. The crowds got even bigger. There was talk of a Portland TV station coming up to do a documentary on the team built around poets. And a DJ even did a rap song about us that they played on the Kelso station a few times.

It was as if we'd revived the town for a while. One day, in spite of the rain, Jen, Lena, Freddie, Mavis, and I were single file on Main/56 again. We looked like a line of ducklings with a basketball. Mavis was up front and passed it back to me, and I bounced it through my legs back to Jen, until it got all the way back to Lena, who took it and ran up to the front. The whole time we were chanting, "Go Jacks, go Jacks, go Jacks."

On the second go-round, when Lena ran up to the front,

she turned to face us all, making us stop. "I have an announcement," she said.

She looked real skinny up there, with the rain flattening her hair and running into her eyes so she had to keep blinking.

"We're all ears," Jen said.

"I got into Williams," Lena said proudly.

Since I was right next to her, I got to hug her first, and soon I felt the others squeezing in. "Way to go, Four-point!" I yelled right in her ear. We all hugged for a few seconds and then broke up into a line again.

"No time to waste," Jen said. "It's onward and upward."

So we started off again, chanting and passing the ball, only every time Lena ran to the front, we gave her an extra shove to show her we were proud.

As we continued up the street, I spied a crowd outside my dad's shop. People with umbrellas were standing on the step and spilling out onto the sidewalk. When we got there, I could see that the place was full. Dad had put a makeshift sign in the window:

## FREE HAIRCUTS

Both of the chairs were occupied. As I got closer, I could see that Vern Castleman had already been in for his. There was a big nick on the side of his head.

"What's going on?" I asked.

"Just like old times," Vern answered.

The team squeezed inside and we stood next to the window. It was humid and smoky, but nobody seemed to mind. Dad had clippers in his hand and was making a mess of Dante

Birmingham, a guy from the '87 team whose shorts came off in the middle of making the game-winning jump shot against Winlock.

"Looking good," my dad said.

But Dante had that frightened look on his face that all my dad's customers get when they go under the scissors.

We'd come in during a conversation about the old days. Darwin, who was waiting his turn, said, "Remember when Dan got his glove caught in the green chain?"

A roar went up and trickled out to the street. The green chain is the conveyor belt that sends rough lumber up to be shaved. Dan, Lena's uncle, had screamed as the belt pulled him up toward the saw. I guess the whole shift sprang into action and tried to cut off the power. But it was my dad who finally did it. Lena's uncle still has the scar on his wrist from where the saw had just begun to bite into his skin.

While the crowd laughed, Lena's uncle waved from the corner of the shop, pointing toward the scar.

"You're welcome, Dan," my dad said.

I leaned back and watched him. I loved seeing the smile on his face, the way he was talking with the same kind of comic flair he used to have. He had an audience, and he was working it. His eyes were bright and sparkling, so different from the beaten man out on the school playground. I looked around for my mom but remembered she was working. She needed to see this.

"You going to take up this haircutting for good?" Stew Schultz asked.

"Sure, Stew, free haircuts. That ought to net me a fortune." He pulled the smock off Dante, and fine bits of hair floated to the floor. "What do you think?" Dad asked.

Dante checked the mirror and shrugged. "You get what you pay for, I guess."

"What *are* you going to do, Buzz?" Darwin asked.

Dad took it in stride, shaking out the smock. "For damn sure you're not going to find me in school with you," he said.

"You can buy my store," Marv Engel said.

"Videos?" said Dad. "I don't have time for that."

Marv looked around the shop. "Anybody interested? I can give you a good price."

It grew quiet. Stew quickly jumped into the empty chair and let Dad pin the smock around his neck. In the silence it felt like we were all melting together, facing the same problem. We weren't talking about it, but we knew it was the mill.

"School might not be so bad," Vern finally said. "All us old dogs could learn a few new tricks."

"And then what do you do?" my dad asked.

Vern cocked his head. "Get different work."

I had a new appreciation for Vern Castleman right then, for all the people crowded inside and outside my dad's shop. Maybe they had been listening to the silence all along. Maybe they knew after all that they would have to make changes. Mavis's parents had made the first move, but now the door was open for everyone else.

"If we get different work," Stew said, "then we're gone from here."

"Use your head, Schultz," Vern said. "Why would that have to happen? You have a car. Did you ever hear the word commute?"

"The only commute Stew makes," said Darwin, "is from his house to one of the Cones."

Even I laughed at that one. It loosened the place up even more. I watched my dad trying to be careful with Stew's hair, but it wasn't working. It was like his mind was someplace else. Maybe he was thinking about what Vern had just said. It was making me wonder about Hemlock. Is your town the place where you work or the place where you live? Maybe it didn't have to be both.

Lena leaned over to me. "I'm getting nervous," she whispered.

"Why?" I said.

"Look what your dad's doing to people's hair. What if it looks like we're standing in line?"

"This isn't the Cut 'n' Curl," I told her. "He doesn't do ladies' hair." I didn't want to leave. It was feeling too good to be around everyone. And I was proud of my dad. He was smiling and laughing like it was the easiest thing in the world to do. People were listening to him tell jokes and stories while he whittled away at what was left of a decent haircut.

But the other girls were growing restless, so Jen finally led us out the door. Some of the guys patted us on the back as we walked out. "Go get 'em, girls," I heard. I think not only my dad but the girls' team too was reminding them of the good times. I felt lighter when we started up our routine again on the street. I felt "Go Jacks" in my legs. And in my heart.

Ever since I'd passed out on the court, Mom was after me about how I was feeling. She became a hovering machine. I'd be putting the finishing touches on a turkey sandwich, and I'd feel her presence behind me.

"Are you sure you don't need me to do that?" she'd offer.

149

"I don't think so."

"Is your hand shaking, darling?" she'd ask.

Which, of course, made me self-conscious of my hands. Seeing I was flustered, she'd back off.

"I was just wondering," she'd say. "Just checking in, as you say."

Finally, one night I said, "How are *you* doing, Mom?"

"Oh, you know. Surviving. Work's the same as always. I'll be getting a few more hours this month, so that'll help."

I took a bite out of the sandwich and started to head for my room, but something about the way Mom was standing there, her shoulders hunched, made me stop.

"Is there something you want to talk about?" I asked.

She shook her head. "No. I don't think so."

I nodded and continued up to my room. I could have done some chemistry or history, but instead I grabbed the poetry book off my desk and lay down on my bed.

Even though I'd been reciting "Because I could not stop for Death" all season, I read it once again. Suddenly, it seemed too sad, too messy. The book had grown worn from my flipping through it practically every day, reading all of Dickinson's poems. And now I realized there were others I liked better, especially the poems that seemed to be more positive.

I knew why I had chosen "Because I could not stop for Death." It had to do with me losing Benny. But every time I recited it, it felt like I was throwing his death right back in my own face. Did I want to make sure I would never forget him? If that was true, it was a mean thing to do to myself.

I was tired and started drifting off. But right when I hit that nice twilight kind of feeling, my mom tapped on the door and peeked in.

"You were right, Brenda," she said. "I do have something to tell you."

"Okay."

She came in and sat on my bed. "Change is hard, isn't it?"

"The worst," I agreed.

She took a deep breath. "I'm going to do something that has me scared."

"You're not divorcing Dad, are you?"

"No," she said, although it wasn't very convincing. "I had a talk with Glenda down at the video store, and she was telling me that she and Marv are thinking of moving. Going to California to be closer to their grandkids. The good part is they want to go right away, and I think they would give me a good deal on the store."

"You want to buy the video store?"

"I'm thinking of it."

"Can we afford it?" I asked.

"They're willing to let me make monthly payments, so yes, I think I might be able to swing it."

"That's great, Mom."

"It is. But I just hate the fact that I have to make a change like this. Your father has no work at the mill, and he's still dragging his feet about what to do. So that leaves me to figure this out." She sniffed and sat up straighter. "But I need to buck up."

"Me too," I said.

She patted me. "We'll buck up together then," she said. "We can't let it keep us down forever. Change is a challenge, and we've made it through a lot of challenges already."

She gathered me in and we held each other. Even though she didn't say it straight out, I knew she was talking about

Benny. It wasn't perfect, but it was all she could do for now. That was a change too. Maybe an even bigger and more difficult change than buying the video store.

I whispered in her ear. "Will I get free videos from your store?"

She laughed. "If you're good," she answered. I hugged her harder. It felt good that Mom and I were in this together. She was trying to make something out of this changed life of hers. And I was too. It was like what Benny had said to me: You couldn't avoid things your whole life. You had to find a way to deal with them. That night my Mom and I started doing just that.

# Chapter 17

The next week we won the league. And we won it by beating the only team that had beaten us: Boistfort. This time there was no Dad staggering out on the court and interfering with our rhythm, and we won by thirteen. Then we powered our way through the first two games at District. We played like the stars we were, every one of us. Only one more game stood between us and State. Unfortunately, it was with Napavine, and they were out for revenge.

There's a rule about rivals playing each other. It doesn't matter how the last game went, or whether it was the week before or even the day before, there is always the chance the other team can win. And it is extremely painful to have your archrival beat you at District.

That week before the Napavine game, all the years of tradition and bragging rights raised their heads and made me nervous. Neighbors were stopping me on the street to tell about a season they almost went to State way back in the fifties or how somebody, who was now dead, once pulled out the game winner in the last second. I realized more than ever how big a responsibility our team carried. It seemed we all got so wound up with the possibility of going to State that we forgot one of our own responsibilities: protecting the tallest tree in Lewis County.

Of course Napavine was out to get us. Who wouldn't be? Everyone enjoys knocking off the big guy. And we were on guard. Our team met at the tree after both games the week before the Friday-night final. And on Thursday we were down there again keeping watch. There weren't very many people out and those who drove by gave us a honk and a thumbs-up. The boys' team was there too, and I found I was happy to see Eric among them. I'd been thinking about him since the night of the Morton game. I hadn't run into him outside school, but all my focus lately had been on basketball anyway.

Jen and Lena were cleaning needles from around the base of the tree, so I pitched in and helped. Lena had her backpack on, and every time she bent over, it would fall off her shoulder and knock the needles out of her hand.

"Hey, Four-point, don't you think you could leave that thing in your car?" Jen asked.

"What if I need to look something up?" said Lena.

"Then you go to the car and look it up."

Lena stood up and adjusted the backpack again. "I feel better when I have it with me," she said.

I glanced up and saw Freddie and Mavis talking with the boys. It all seemed so normal. Maybe it was the first time I'd felt normal in a long time. "I like this," I said.

"Like what?" Lena asked.

"This. The whole town coming together, no worries, no changes. Just the way it always was."

"Yeah," Jen said. "The way it was. Remember when we couldn't buy a win in this league?"

"Maybe," I said. "But if losing a few games would bring everything back, I'd go for that."

"I might too," Lena said quietly.

Jen threw her handful of needles at the two of us. "You mean, you'd give up the chance to go to State just so everything would stay the same?"

"Oh, you like the way it's going now?" I challenged her.

"What's wrong with a little change in this town?" she asked. "Tell the truth. Do the two of you want to grow up, get married, have kids, and die here without anything being different?"

"I don't want that," I said. "I just like it being the same once in a while."

"What about you, Lena?" Jen asked. "You don't really think you're going to go off to some big-time eastern college and then come back to Hemlock, do you?"

The look on Lena's face said she had expected to do just that.

Jen shook her head as she bent to gather more needles. "I mean, you could really be somebody," she said.

"I am somebody," Lena said. "And what about you? Are you going to college?"

"Maybe," Jen said. She straightened up and looked at me, raising her eyebrows.

"You should," Lena said. "You're perfectly capable. Maybe if you go away, you'll see that Hemlock isn't such a bad place after all."

"Whatever," Jen said. She put her hands on her hips and looked around. "Nobody's coming to chop down this tree. I say we go home."

We all piled into Jen's car, and she dropped us off, one by one. I was the last one, and when we got to my house, she and I sat in the car for a minute.

"What was that about, back there with Lena?" I asked.

"What?"

"The whole college thing. You were kind of hard on her."

"Lena's naive."

"All right, Jen. Out with it. What's up with you?"

She took a deep breath and blew it out slowly. "I don't know for sure. All I know is I have this fluttering feeling in my stomach all the time. I thought when I rejoined the team that would take care of it. But it's still there. I don't know what it means."

"When did it start?"

"Ever since my name was in the Seattle paper. No matter what I do, this feeling won't go away."

I thought about what Benny had told me. "Maybe something's bothering you that you need to talk about."

She looked at me like I was from another planet. "You've been watching too much Oprah again."

"Quit it, Jen. You know what I'm saying."

I expected a fight, but she only shrugged. "I'm just not myself anymore"

"Nobody is, Jen. Look at everyone in Hemlock. You heard them at my dad's shop."

"I was lying back at the tree," she said. "I don't want things to change, either. But at the same time I do. I think you know what I'm talking about."

"Do you think the other girls feel it too?" I asked.

"Well, Freddie seems quieter than usual. Mavis is still

freaked about her folks leaving town. We know Lena feels it." Jen turned to me. "I'll tell you what I'm really scared about. It's the future."

"Me too," I said.

"Like, where will you and I be twenty years from now? What will we be doing?"

"Even ten years from now," I said.

"Five."

"Next year," I said.

"Jeez, tomorrow." She laughed then, and I joined in. There were a lot of nerves jumping around in the air.

"I'm really going to miss you," I said.

"You're going down to Oregon, aren't you?" she said.

"Yeah," I answered. "I haven't heard from Washington yet, but I talked to a coach at Oregon. It's looking good."

"Think about it, Bren. You'll be in a big-time program, working your butt off. And getting a big-time education. Think of all the people you'll meet. People who aren't from around here."

"Listen," I said, "I saw that look you threw me when Lena was talking about college. And you said maybe. Have you talked with Ms. Cochran?"

"Once. But I haven't really followed up on it."

"Does she still want you to play at her college?"

"She did. She was big on it."

"Then why haven't you followed up on it? Maybe that's why your stomach's aching. Because you haven't."

"But—"

"There you go again. Finding reasons not to. Jen, you need to get ahold of her. What are you waiting for?"

"I'm waiting for my stomach to quit aching," she said.

"Do it," I said. "I don't know for sure, but I think it might be better to be down there with an aching belly than up here waiting for it to stop."

"Well, aren't you the amateur shrink these days," she said, back to her old self.

"I'm going to miss you, Jen."

"If I do go to Oregon, do you promise we'll meet up sometimes?"

"Promise. I'll probably be wanting to more than you." Before I left the car, I added, "I'm going to make sure you call Ms. Cochran, Jen. I think you need to take control of what you can and forget about the things you have no control over."

"Like what?" she said.

"Like your own life, for one."

In the house I sat on my bed and thought about the team, especially Jen. There was no getting around the fact that with each passing day, something was coming closer for all of us. Maybe that's what Benny had meant that time in the locker room, when he said, "Something's coming. Won't be long now." What was coming was an ending. The end of an era for all of us. And the only thing to do was to latch onto the new era and hold it tight.

# Chapter 18

On the day of the district final, I went into Benny's room to borrow his socks again. But when I turned on the light in the closet, the box wasn't there. I looked around, even under his bed, but it was nowhere to be found.

I called Mom upstairs, but she didn't like going into Benny's room, so she stood in the doorway.

"Your father took it," she said.

"You let him?"

"Yes. Benny was his son."

"But this is his room," I wailed.

"You don't have to make a fuss about it, Bren. You can go down to the shop and ask your father if you can look through the box."

"But I still don't understand why you let him take it."

"Brenda." My mom took me by the shoulders and made me look in her eyes. "Your father is having a hard time with this. He's a little frayed around the edges right now. To be honest, I don't need the stuff he would dish out if I tried to stop him. If you want the box, you'll have to go deal with him."

If it hadn't been tournament time, I wouldn't have gotten up the guts to go down to the shop. District is make or break. If you don't survive there, you don't go to State, and if you don't go to State, well, your season's over. I decided that a potential state champion should not be afraid of talking to her father.

When I got there, my dad was cutting Stan Schultz's hair. As soon as I walked in, I could see the trademark gouge on the left side of Stan's head, above his ear. Dad was in the process of trying to cover it over with hair from the top.

"Brenda, Brenda, Brenda," Stan said. "Fit as a fiddle and twice as tall."

"Hi, Dad," I said.

He smiled and nodded. "How's that noggin?"

"Better."

"Should have beat the stuffing out of whoever did that to you," Stan said.

My dad cuffed him on the side of the head. "Shut up, Stan. She fell, remember? Just look straight ahead and don't open your mouth." It's always amazed me the way people do what my dad tells them. Stan closed his mouth and looked straight ahead at the mirror.

I had butterflies, but I went ahead. "I was looking for something," I said.

"Yeah?"

"Yeah. Mom said you took some of Benny's stuff from his room."

The scissors got very loud then. And pretty close to Stan's ear. I saw him flinch.

"That Benny—" Stan tried.

"I said shut up," my dad reminded him. "What are you after, Bren?"

I straightened up, but when I was around my father, I never felt as tall as I was. "I want to look through his stuff."

The scissors stopped. Dad stood there with them open right above Stan's ear. "Why?"

I glanced at Stan. "Could I talk to you in private, Dad?"

"I've got a customer," he said as he started clipping again. Behind me the bell on the front door jingled and Stew Schultz came in. He walked right past me without saying anything and inspected Stan's haircut.

"Looks like hell," said Stew.

"You try and do better," Dad said.

Didn't it matter that I was standing right there? Were the Schultz twins more important to my dad than I was? I was tired of it. No more shadows for me. I walked past them all and went into the back apartment.

The place was a mess. Half of Dad's clothes were crumpled on the floor, and beer cans sprinkled with cigarette ash covered the coffee table. I went over to the closet and started tossing things over my shoulder. And just as I saw Benny's box in the corner, something else caught my eye.

"What are you doing?" my dad asked behind me. I snapped up so fast, I banged my head on the door.

"You okay?" Dad asked.

I rubbed the sore spot, but that only made it hurt worse. "Yes, I'm okay."

"What are you after?"

"Dad, what's this?" I said. As I pulled Mr. Hobbs's hat out of the closet, I felt the same quaking as that day on the school playground.

"What does it look like?"

"But what's it doing in your closet?"

He took it from me and examined it. "I think one of the Schultzes brought it here. Hell, I don't know. What difference does it make?"

"It belongs to my coach. It was taken the night he was beat up. Remember that night?"

"Are you accusing me of something, Brenda?"

"No." Having him so close was throwing me off. "I just want to borrow Benny's socks," I said.

"His socks? What for?"

"For luck," I said.

I knew right away he didn't like the idea. "Well, you can't say they really brought him much luck, can you?"

"That's a horrible thing to say, Dad."

He shrugged. "Life ain't nice."

"So is it okay?"

"I don't know, Brenda," he said. "Maybe we should leave them be. The school might want to put them in the trophy case or something."

It might have been the casual way he said it, but I snapped. "Why are you this way?" I yelled.

"What way?"

"This way," I said, motioning to the room. I could feel sweat on my forehead, and my voice revved up. "You hang around drunks and treat them like your best friends. You act like

162

you're blind to everything going on in this town. You get into trouble so you can't come to any of my ball games. And for all I know, you beat up my coach." I could feel the anger building, but this time I couldn't keep it in. "And you treat me like you don't even know me. Like I don't matter to you."

"Hold on now, Brenda," he said, throwing down Mr. Hobbs's hat.

"No, Dad, I'm not holding on. Not anymore."

I saw his face get red, and his lips drew into a sneer. "I lost my only son, Brenda!" he snapped.

"Well, you're about to lose me too!" I yelled. "What am I to you anyway? You used to be nice to me when Benny was around. I didn't die, Dad. Get it? I'm still here."

I could feel the air pumping in and out of my lungs. My feelings were overpowering; I just wanted to hit him and hit him and hit him. If he had said one more word, I might have done it. But he just stood there, his face red, his jaw clenched. I quickly leaned down, grabbed Mr. Hobbs's hat, and left the shop. I never wanted to speak to him again.

I wasn't feeling any better that night. I got to the locker room early and dressed quickly for the game. In the gym I found Mr. Hobbs on the bench, going over scouting reports for the teams from other leagues. I held out his hat.

"I believe this is yours," I said.

He studied it for a moment before he took it. "Where . . . ?"

"It doesn't matter," I said.

"What is it, Brenda?" he said as he put on the hat. "You don't sound like yourself."

I shook my head. "What gives you the right to know who I

sound like or who I don't sound like? And take that thing off, will you?" I snatched the hat and threw it up into the bleachers. I couldn't bear to see the hurt look on his face, so I turned and ran out of the gym and into the night.

It was cold, but it didn't much matter. I walked over to the big field behind the gym and just kept going. When I got a hundred yards or so, I stopped and turned. The gym looked like a big ocean liner, all lit up on a calm sea. A row of tall meshed windows threw light over the grass, and a fire escape on one end zigzagged up to the windows. It looked like someone was up there, peeking through the glass.

But all I could focus on was my breathing. The familiar pain in my gut was back, and my chest was hurting too. I was about to just lie down in the field and drift away peacefully, when something moved beside me. I turned and there was Benny. He was all dressed for a game.

"You," I said.

"The one and only."

I blew out a ragged breath. "You should have seen me just now in there," I said. "I was acting like Dad. Like a spoiled little brat."

"Interesting," he said. "Like father, like daughter, huh?"

"No, it's not like that at all. I don't ever want to be like him."

"But it makes sense that you might be a little like him, Bren. You are his daughter."

"Well, it doesn't feel right. Poor Mr. Hobbs."

"It's okay," he said. "Once in a while everybody blows their stack. It doesn't mean it's a permanent part of your personality."

"I just want to be myself. Can't you see that? I want to be Brenda."

He laughed. "That's a good one, Bren."

"What's so funny?"

"Because I'll bet you anything you don't know who Brenda is yet. Do you?"

It wasn't hard to answer, and it made me feel humble. "Not really. I just know I don't want to do things like Dad does."

"You don't usually do things like he does."

We walked farther into the darkness. It seemed colder now, and I rubbed at my arms. "You were right, Benny," I said.

"About what?"

"About getting it all out. I feel better."

"Are you sure you've gotten it all out?"

I stopped. "No. Not all of it. But I don't really know where to go from here. Do you have any ideas?"

"Sorry. I don't have all the answers. But I think the important thing is you should always be ready for what comes along. Keep in practice, because sometimes life will call you in off the bench."

"I don't remember you being such a big-time philosopher," I said. We started walking again. "There is something I've been wanting to ask you, Benny."

"Okay, shoot."

"Why didn't you just come home that night?"

"You think that's how it works? You think I should have just gone home after the game so everything would be fine?"

"I don't know how it works. That's why I'm asking you."

"I think you do know, Brenda. You're smarter than you give yourself credit for."

"Okay, then. You didn't come home because you felt like you were old enough to do things on your own. You just felt good, and you wanted to be with your friends, and you wanted to go over every detail of the game, and you wanted to laugh about the stupid things and hear other guys say how well you played. You needed to do that."

"See, you do know after all. It's what seniors do, Brenda. It's normal. So what you're really asking me is how come I had to be so normal."

I clenched my fists. "Can't you just talk straight to me for a change?"

"Calm down, will you?" he said. "It's about leaving home. Little by little, you've got to let go of it. One day you can't let go of Mommy's hand, and the next you just want to hang out with your friends. Pretty soon you don't live there anymore."

"It's hard doing this without you."

"I know, Bren. I'm sorry."

I was feeling tired, as if it was draining my energy just to keep my brother out there with me in the field. "I don't want to do this anymore," I said.

"Do what? Play basketball?"

"No. I don't want to feel this way anymore."

"What way?"

"Bad. I don't want this to be the way it is. I hate that you're gone. That I can never watch you play again. That Mom and Dad may never get back together. That I might not see my friends again after this year. It's too much."

"Then do what you told Jen to do. Take care of the things you can. You can't change the fact that the mill closed. You can't change that I died. Why worry about those things if you can't change them?"

"But I want so bad to be able to do something about them."

"You can, Bren. Only you can't open the mill and you can't bring me back to life. You can't turn the years back. You are going to graduate and you are going to leave town. Accept it. What you can do is step out of the rain and into the sunshine and live your life."

I felt the tears coming, so I turned away from him.

"It's hard to be the one everyone looks at."

It was his voice, but I felt my own lips saying it: "It's hard to be the one everyone looks at." Like I was really only talking to myself.

I turned back and he was gone. Instead, I saw only the gym all lit up for the big game. It called to me, drew me to it like a magnet. As I walked back, I went over in my head what we'd talked about, especially the part about letting things go. Was he talking about him too? Goose bumps rose on my skin. Would I have to let him go? I wondered if that was true about anyone you lose. Are you ever ready to say goodbye? Do the memories ever stop coming? Or will the day come when Benny's name just stops rolling off my tongue?

Soon I could hear balls bouncing inside the gym. I was sure Mr. Hobbs was having a conniption about where I was. As I passed by the fire escape, I looked up. Someone was standing there, and I cocked my head to get a better view through the bars.

"Dad?"

He might have been banned from inside the gyms, but there he was, up on the landing, shading his eyes to see through the mesh window. He jumped back at the sound of my voice.

"What are you doing up there?"

He turned and started climbing down the ladder, stopping a few feet above me. "Just looking," he said. He dug into his coat pocket and pulled out Benny's socks. "I decided you might need these after all."

As I took them from him, I said, "How many games have you been to?"

"Don't know," he said. "Pretty much all of them."

"Why didn't you tell me?"

"I'm not much for those kinds of words, Brenda. You know that."

"I've got to get inside," I said, holding up the socks.

"Put them to good use," he said. And then he started climbing back up the ladder.

# Chapter 19

It was loud and crazy inside the gym. Just the way I like it. Mr. Hobbs was so happy to see me back, he jumped up and down like a little kid. I noticed the old hat was back on his head, and I have to admit I was almost happy to see it. He came over as I sat down on the bench to change my socks.

"Miss Dickinson," he started.

"Forget what I said."

"You were right, though," he said. "I shouldn't have assumed to know how you were feeling. Nobody knows what it's like for you."

It was just what I needed to hear. I felt calmer and focused. "Thanks, Mr. Hobbs."

I tore out on the floor and caught the last couple minutes of warm-up. I was ready for anything. Benny was in my socks and my dad was hiding on the fire escape. It was almost like the good old days.

Napavine was out for blood. One of their forwards had a

smirk on her face that said she planned to rip Mavis to shreds, and their center was giving me a dirty look. Mr. Hobbs huddled us together and reminded us it was only psychological and that we were way beyond paying attention to that.

As we stepped onto the court, I surveyed the gym. There weren't nearly as many Napavine fans there as you'd expect for a district game. Meanwhile, our stands were packed, and the usual group sat ready with their little signs. Jen had said it was the nerds' time to shine. All those people who had kept to themselves and loved poetry in the privacy of their bedrooms were out, showing the rest of the world how much they knew about rhyme.

At the tip I felt a spring in my feet. I floated above the other girl and swatted the ball back to Freddie. I knew what was going to happen that game. I felt it everywhere, and I was right. We won going away, 64–47. Mr. Hobbs took me out in the last minute, and I got a standing ovation. Then I joined the rest of the starters on the bench and we chanted, "On to State, On to State, On to State . . ." until our voices gave out. When the buzzer went off, we made a mad dash to the middle of the floor and fell into a giggling heap.

The crowd pushed in on us as the band played "We Are the Champions" over and over again. My mom dumped popcorn on the heads of the nearest parents. I found myself hugging people I'd never thought of touching before. For those few minutes after the game everybody in Hemlock was family. I was absolutely sure there was no one left in town.

In the locker room we showered and dressed with so much commotion, it seemed like a heavy metal concert. We were completely out of character that night. We usually took time to dry our hair and fix ourselves up, but there we were with our hair wet and stringy, singing and screaming and joking around. But over on the bench, Jen was sitting alone, staring at the floor. Her lips were moving, but nothing was coming out.

I slipped away from the rest of the team and knelt down in front of Jen. "What?" I said. She looked up at me and whispered, but I couldn't make it out. "Are you okay?"

She nodded. Then the whisper got louder. She seemed to be rapping something about the team. I strained to listen more closely. The other girls stopped and listened too.

> *"Young and old, come hear this sound,*
> *Listen to the rhyme I'm setting down. . . ."*

At first I thought my craziness was catching, but Jen stood up with the biggest smile I'd ever seen on her face. Then her voice got louder.

> *"You can't win if you lose, can't lose if you win,*
> *Bound for a glory that will never end."*

Behind her, Freddie took up the beat. The other girls started slapping their legs, tapping their feet.

> *"From the south to the north, from the east to the west,*
> *Hemlock girls, they are the best."*

It was a goofy rhyme and I knew Jen was making it up as she went along, but I jumped up and started clapping.

171

> *"The end is the start, the start is the end,*
> *A three-point score I'm about to send."*

Then it was my turn.

> *"Endless, boundless, goes for miles,*
> *Stoking up the fire for the final trials."*

It was like nothing bad had ever happened in our lives. The team stood around in a circle. We leaned in and put our arms around one another's shoulders. When one person was through with her contribution, we chanted it all over again.

> *"Endless, boundless, goes for miles,*
> *Stoking up the fire for the final trials."*

The rhythm took over our bodies. It made us want to get on the drums, to dance until we dropped. We didn't plan the song, but it was as if we had.

We'd never have made it past the first round of any talent contest. It was like the flu; it was an epidemic of insanity. A contagious spirit passed from Jen to me to Mavis to Freddie to Lena, and to every other girl in the room. Jen and I broke away, and she started kicking her legs out, like a Rockette.

> *"Then I saw the basket, waiting for my shot*
> *Cutting through the air like a missile hot."*

Jen turned away, and I grabbed her waist from behind. Then Mavis latched onto me, Freddie onto Mavis, and the rest of the team after that, until we were one big conga line. We were a bunch of girls in one long girl chain, and we loved it.

There are times when it doesn't matter who sees you, and this was one of those moments. We snaked through the locker room, forest girls doing a really bad version of urban music. I was laughing so hard, I could barely sing, but I gave it my best. We sounded like a punch-drunk girls' chorus that hadn't had much practice.

"*Heads up, heads up, we'll dribble through you,*" we sang. But it wasn't enough to just do it in the locker room. Jen led us down the hall, and we burst through the doors and into the gym, where our families started clapping for us.

"*Heads up, heads up, we'll pass through you.*"

Mr. Hobbs had his hands together over his head in a victory salute. Eric was at the back of the crowd, clapping along with everybody else. He winked at me, and I yelled even louder. I was thinking that this was the single greatest moment of my life. But I was wrong. There was another, even better one on the way.

Outside, the crowd was still clapping. It was cold, and a cloud of frosty breath hung above them. To the rear my dad was putting his hands together too, and I walked over to him.

"You played a great game," he said.

"We're going to State, Dad!" I put my arms around him and felt him squeeze me back.

"How about that?" he said. I looked at his face and saw the pain. I wasn't the one who was supposed to take us to State.

"Good job," he added. Then he slid his hands into his pockets and walked away.

As the crowd grew thinner, Eric materialized by my side. "It's cold," he said.

"My dad's not doing well," I told him. "I don't know what to do about it. And I probably shouldn't be telling you this because of the way our dads feel about each other."

"Don't worry. Your secret's safe with me."

I had a feeling it would be safe with Eric. Maybe any secret would be.

It wasn't long before the International drove by with my dad at the wheel and the Schultz twins sitting next to him. Mom's Monte Carlo sputtered along behind them.

Mom rolled down the window. "You'll miss the bus," she said.

"I don't think I'm going on the bus," I said. "It's okay. I'll be home in a little while."

She gave us the once-over and then rolled up the window and took off.

"Well, what do you think?" Eric said.

"I just want to go."

"Where?" he said.

"It doesn't really matter. Do you mind if we just drive around?"

He reached for my gym bag, but he was all thumbs and fumbled with it before he hefted it up on his shoulder.

At his car he put my bag in the back and then held the door open for me. How bad could his parents be if they had trained their son so well? It was freezing in his car, so I put my hands between my knees. Eric turned on the heat before pulling out of the parking lot.

As we drove, I watched the trees go by. In some places they hung over the roadway, and in the dark they looked like long needly arms trying to swing down and touch us. Almost as if they were human. There's a story that a great-grandma of mine went a little loony when her husband was killed in a logging accident. She went around town trying to cut down all the trees she could find because she blamed them for her husband's death. I can understand how someone might see them as alive. When it comes down to it, a tree killed my brother.

No one was out on the road now. The car's headlights flashed on the road markers and little sparkling eyes waiting in the bushes. The inside of the car grew warm, and I released my hands from between my knees. But I didn't exactly know what to do with them. I was suddenly very conscious of Eric sitting so close to me.

We finally got close to town. "Pull over," I said.

His headlights shone on the sign at the town limits.

"If your brother was still alive . . . ," he said.

"If my brother was still alive, what?"

"I don't know. The sign might be different now."

"You think?"

"Maybe." He took a deep breath and said, "Not that it matters much. Basketball isn't all that important."

"Uh, right about now it's pretty darn important to me," I said.

He laughed. "I know. But maybe not in the big picture. There's more to life than sports. What are we going to do when we're old like our parents? Come out here to see the contribution we made to Hemlock? That's not what I want to do."

I stared at the sign. "You may be right about that," I said. "It's even worse that there is no ninth place."

"Everybody knows that."

"So why do you think my grandpa had this sign made?"

"You won't like what I think."

"Try me."

"I think whoever decided to put this sign up had no hope for the future. I mean, think about it. There is no ninth place, but they decided to say there was. My guess is they didn't think anyone would ever do better. If you ask me, it's a curse."

As much as I felt myself wanting to stand up for my grandfather, what Eric was saying made sense. "I've never looked at it that way before," I said.

"Me, neither, till just now."

The inside of the car grew quiet. I liked that about him; he didn't seem to mind if it was quiet too long. You notice your life more without all that noise getting in the way.

I felt relaxed. I stopped looking at the sign and checked out the inside of his car again. It was starting to feel kind of homey. I was beginning to realize there might be a lot of homes for me outside my own.

"Eric," I said, "did I ever thank you for talking to me at Benny's funeral?"

"I didn't exactly do it so you'd have to say thanks," he said.

"Well, just in case I didn't, I want to thank you."

"You're welcome," he said. "Want to hear my secret? When I talked to you that time, my hands were sweaty and my heart was practically zooming out of my chest."

"Just because you were talking to me?" I asked, surprised.

"Yeah. I liked you even then." He laughed nervously.

I felt a warmth in my chest, instead of the tightness I'd been feeling the last few weeks. And I was thinking I must have liked him then too. I'd always admired the way he seemed to know so much about everything in the classes we shared. Until now, though, he'd never seemed like the kind of guy I would spend time at the sign with. But here we were, and I didn't care who came by to see. Not my mom, not even my dad. I could make up my own mind about who I wanted to spend time with.

My hand crept across the seat and found his. He grasped it tightly. "I did feel like you were my friend then, Eric," I said.

"I was. I just wasn't sure if you'd want to be friends with a Jolley."

I sat back, still holding his hand. I thought of my own parents at the Fostoria lot before they were married. They were my age, thinking about their future. How wide open it was. How excited they must have been. No sign of loss in sight. *"Rage, rage against the dying of the light,"* I whispered.

"What was that?" he asked.

"Just a poem," I said. I scooted over close to him, and he put his arm around my shoulder. I closed my eyes and felt his lips brush against mine.

When we came up for air, I said, "I think we're about to change how this town thinks about the Jolleys and the Jacobsens."

He squeezed me and then reached down and turned off the headlights. At least for that night, neither of us cared about the sign anymore.

On the way home we drove by the mill. It looked as cold and dark as it had since it closed. I turned and watched as it disappeared through the back window. I tried to frame it like a picture in my mind so I would never forget.

"Now what?" Eric said.

I turned back around and saw red lights flashing in the middle of town. My stomach tightened up as we got closer. It was a sheriff's car, its lights twirling in the dark. But when I saw what had happened, I thought it should have been an ambulance.

I pressed in closer to Eric as we drove by slowly, taking care to avoid all the people standing in the street. It was so sad. They were gathered around what had been the tallest tree in Lewis County. It was now cut in two, the top half lying in the grass in front of City Hall.

# Chapter 20

When those Napavine thugs cut down the tallest tree in Lewis County, they might as well have cut a piece out of everybody's heart. The whole town filed by to see the mighty hemlock lying in state in the City Hall parking lot. I could feel my focus slipping away, and the whole team's morale plummet.

"But you're going to State," Mom said. "Doesn't that matter to you?"

"They cut down the tree" was all I said to that.

Mr. Hobbs called a team meeting. "The timing of this is awfully bad," he said. "I believe the individual or individuals who perpetrated this act are under the impression that it will affect your play. But as I look around at your earnest faces, I see they couldn't be more wrong."

I don't know what faces he was looking at. The ones I noticed looked pretty glum. We were like the smokestacks at the mill—no steam left.

Only Jen was riled. "I say we head over to Napavine, find out who did it, and make sure they won't be doing it again."

"Violence is not the answer," Mr. Hobbs said. But I'm not sure he had many takers on that one.

On the plus side, we got write-ups in the papers in Longview and Tacoma and another one in the Seattle paper. The one in Longview even had a picture of us doing our Lumberjill Rap, as the caption called it. There was a mixed reaction in the area. Basketball diehards called us a sham. "You can't treat basketball like some weird reality show. Making things rhyme doesn't translate to respect for the game. They won't last more than two days at State." Another person asked, "Isn't there a rule that says you can't talk at the foul line?" I guess when you're successful, there's always someone around who wants to bring you down.

Since we'd won District on Friday night, Saturday was a free day for us. We could go back over to the gym and watch the consolation games or just relax before leaving for Spokane on Monday. As much as I loved watching other teams play, I wasn't in the mood to take in a game. But the rest of the team wanted to go, so there I was two days before leaving for State, all alone in Hemlock.

Except for Darwin Ostrander, who was standing by himself in front of City Hall. He was reaching up to touch one of the cuts in the tree.

It was a hideous scar. They'd taken about fifteen feet off the top, but it looked like they'd hacked at it lower down too. There were big bites showing white tree flesh up and down the trunk. I wondered how they'd gotten away with it, but then I remembered how empty the Napavine side of the bleachers had been the night before.

I walked up to Darwin and realized he'd been crying. His eyes were red and puffy. A big lump formed in my throat to see him that way.

"You okay?" I asked.

He nodded. "This baby isn't, though." He touched the trunk again. "Who could do something like this?"

"Napavine," I said.

"But why?"

I felt a twinge of guilt. "Because we shaved the top off theirs."

He walked around the tree, sighing deeply and gently touching the cuts here and there. "So I guess this means it's not the tallest tree in Lewis County anymore."

"Theirs is taller now," I said. "It's not right."

"Why aren't you over watching the other games?" he asked.

"I don't much feel like it," I said. I think I was staring at him too much, because he seemed to get nervous.

"Did you want something?" he asked.

By reflex I looked around to make sure the coast was clear. "I saw Benny again," I said.

"'Course you did." He was so matter-of-fact.

"But why?"

"I thought we went over this," he said.

"But why then? I felt good. We were at District."

"And I'm at community college. Things are looking up. Why do I see Margie every night before I go to bed?"

I didn't say what crossed my mind: because you're crazy, Darwin. The thing is, he no longer seemed crazy, despite his affection for the downed tree. I took him by the arm and led him over to the rock wall, where we both sat down.

"It's getting weirder, Darwin." I explained how it seemed

Benny's voice was now my voice; his words, my words. "Does that mean I'm getting worse?"

"You mean, does it make you mentally ill? Hardly. You want to see really crazy, you hang out at Steilacoom for a couple of months, like I did."

"So I'm doomed to see my brother's ghost the rest of my life?"

"Who's talking about ghosts?" Darwin said, a little louder than I would have liked. Then he whispered. "It's not a ghost."

"Sorry," I whispered back.

"A real smart doctor at the hospital told me something I've never forgotten. You want to hear it?"

"I want to hear everything you have to tell me."

"Listen up. The guy asked me, 'Darwin, whenever you talk to your wife who passed away, does she ever tell you anything you don't already know? Does she ever give you any new information?'"

"And what did you say?"

"Well, I had to think about it for a while, but the plain truth was no, she didn't tell me anything new. She didn't tell me anything from the great beyond. She wasn't able to tell me secrets from the past or anything about my future. She just talked about everyday things. She said things like 'You didn't give away that green dress of mine, did you?' or 'You remember when the two of us snuck out of class and went up to Government Camp?' Things we both knew about."

"And what did the doctor say that meant?"

He smiled. "It means it's all coming from inside you. You're not hearing voices or seeing things that don't make sense. You're just hearing you talking to yourself. You're just seeing what you wish you had." He cleared his throat and looked me in the eye. "Don't you want to see Benny, Brenda? Don't you want to hear his voice?"

I nodded. "Anybody would. But it hurts at the same time."

"'Course it does."

I looked at the fallen tree and thought about the times I'd seen Benny. Maybe Darwin's doctor at the hospital was right. Benny hadn't told me anything I didn't already know.

"Haven't you ever wanted it to go away, Darwin?" I asked.

He looked totally surprised. "Now, why would I want it to?"

Right then in front of City Hall, I saw Darwin as the lonely man he was. A sad man who might never get over his loss. Someone resigned to caress the bleeding cuts on a hemlock tree. It was then I knew I had a different answer to the question I'd put to him. And I didn't feel all that guilty, either.

"I love my brother and always have," I said, "But when I see Benny now, it's hard to see around him. I don't know what's beyond him. Sometimes I'd like to know what the rest of my life is going to look like."

I wondered if my dad was going to come over to the tournament in Spokane. He wasn't banned from the arena over there, so he could be sitting in the stands with everyone else. But Spokane was where his team had lost twenty years ago. Maybe he wouldn't want to return to the scene of the crime. When Mom came home from work, I asked her about it.

"He hasn't told me whether he's going or not," she said. "Your father's stuck back in the eighties, and he needs help getting unstuck."

"How's that going to happen, Mom?" I asked.

"I sure wish I knew. But I've got a life to lead myself now, and it doesn't involve following your dad around. I'm afraid that's his problem."

"I don't want you two to split up," I said.

"I don't either, honey. All I'm saying is that the clock keeps ticking no matter what you do. I've got things in the works. And so do you."

She told me about her plans for Spokane. She and some other parents had reserved motel rooms way in advance so there wouldn't be any last-minute problems. Our team would be staying downtown at the Doubletree. Someone from the Boistfort team who went to State the year before said the Doubletree had the cutest bellhops. That might not be the reason we were staying there, but we liked the idea.

We had a light practice on Sunday and were set to go over to Spokane the next day. We were a little clunky on the court, but we were loose, and that's important when you're going into tournament week.

Mr. Hobbs must have had an exceptional attack of nerves, because he called another team meeting after practice. He recited a few sonnets, supposedly to calm us down, but he was pacing back and forth so much that they didn't come out much like sonnets.

"Now, ladies," he said. "You're about to embark on one of the tangled moments of your young lives. You'll need your finest concentration skills. You'll need a pure focus. You'll need to sleep, eat, and dream the bottom of the net. I would implore you at this time to speak up if there is anything that is troubling you, anything that might get in the way of your accomplishing your mission this week. The bus ride over to Spokane? The tree?"

We looked at one another. I thought a few of the girls spent too much time looking at me, but I was mulling over something I needed to say to Mr. Hobbs, so I ignored them.

"If there is any leftover business, let's get it out now. If Mr. Lindsay is mad at Mr. Blake, let's hear it. If Miss Dickinson fears the criticism of Mr. Frost, put it on the table. It's okay to have these feelings," he said. "But let's not keep them to ourselves."

No one said anything, so we broke up after a few minutes. I waited until everyone had gone; then I went into Mr. Hobbs's office. "What you said out there," I said. "Maybe there is something."

"I thought there might be, Emily."

"Do you think I could be Brenda for a sec?"

He smiled and motioned to the chair.

There was no easy way to get it out, so I just forged ahead. "You didn't say anything about the hat," I began.

"I meant to thank you," he said.

"No, I mean you didn't ask any questions about where I got it."

"Now, Brenda, that's all over with, isn't it? It doesn't matter where you got it."

"It matters to me, Mr. Hobbs."

He picked up a pencil and chewed on the end of it. "Sometimes it makes more sense not to say anything about an incident. Here in Hemlock, I mean. There are times when you have to pick and choose your battles and not get your weapon out every time someone does you wrong."

"It doesn't seem fair."

"To you, perhaps. From your perspective. But from mine I can see what motivates people to do things."

185

"What would motivate anyone to do what they did to you?"

"Envy, perhaps."

"With all due respect, Mr. Hobbs, why would anyone envy you?"

He laughed. "Well, certainly on the surface it would seem that I wouldn't engender envy in anyone in this town. But in the big picture of life it may be a different story."

I could tell he was stalling, so I kept quiet and waited.

"My dear Brenda," he finally said. "Everyone wants to be able to accomplish what he or she sets out to do. And accomplish it successfully. I sat on the bench next to Ms. Cochran for years, dreaming that one day I would be able to lead this team. I knew it was most likely a fantasy, but I can tell you that it kept me going for all those years when I felt like leaving this town and pursuing a dream somewhere else. The unfortunate events of the last year conspired to put me in the driver's seat, and now look at me. The coach of the first Hemlock girls' team to go to State. It's not so much that all the other men in this town would like to be in my shoes, but it may be that they are envious that I have had the opportunity to fulfill my dream."

In spite of his hat, in spite of his stubbornness about the poets, Mr. Hobbs seemed smart to me then, smart in a different way. About the world, maybe. "I'm glad you have the opportunity now, Mr. Hobbs."

"I hope someday to hear what your dream is, Brenda," he said.

"I'm not sure I'm ready, Mr. Hobbs."

"Ah, but there's the rub, my dear. Life, as they say, may be ready for you."

# Chapter 21

The night we cut off the top of the Napavine tree, it wasn't actually anybody's idea. Jen says it was her idea because she did the sawing, but Freddie says it was hers and Lena says she thought of it the week before. Mavis took a little credit, and I did too. But really it just all came together at the right time. That's why, when the team met out at the Fostoria Mill the night before we left for State, nobody really knew whose idea it was.

It was clear and cold out. We all dragged over branches and sticks and then collected rocks, forming a circle. Maybe it was the poets speaking to our unconscious, maybe not. But we lit a big fire on the grounds of the Fostoria Mill and sat around it as if we were at camp. Nine girls from Hemlock, Washington, with a wish that would carry us all the way across the state and into our own town's history books.

"I never thought this would happen," Jen said. "I never

thought we'd make it this far. When Ms. Cochran quit, I thought we were doomed."

"Me too," said Freddie. "I thought it then and I thought it even more when you quit the team."

"I didn't quit the team."

"Yes, you did," said Lena.

"I missed a couple of practices."

"You quit, Jen," I said. "Then you came back. It's okay."

She looked like she was going to put up a fight but then just poked at the fire with a stick. "You think they'll come out here, thinking the place is up in flames?" she asked.

"Probably," Freddie said. "Then all our parents will come running to save the mill, and they'll just find us."

"Then they'll tell us to put out the fire," Lena said. "Because it's dangerous and we're too young to be playing with anything dangerous."

"Do you think they'll ever stop treating us like babies?" Jen asked.

"Mine already have stopped," Mavis said. "'Course, they're not exactly here to keep track of me."

"But are we grown up?" Freddie asked.

"It depends," said Lena, "on what your definition is."

"When you're stable in life, like an adult," Freddie said.

Lena laughed. "From what I can see, not too many adults are stable around here. And in the poems I read, people seem to have up-and-down lives. Sometimes they act like children, sometimes more like adults."

"You read too much poetry," Jen said.

"I'm reading it too," Freddie admitted. "And you know what? I kind of like Edna."

"You do?" Jen said.

"Yeah. I wasn't so sure at first, but she's grown on me."

"How?" I asked.

"It's almost like she's with me when I'm standing at the foul line. And it sounds cool to be reciting poetry up there."

"It sounds even cooler when I'm not at the line," Lena said. "Anybody else learn other poems by your poet?"

We glanced at one another, fire flickering off our faces. I realized we looked different in this light. Older maybe. Or wiser.

"I did," Jen admitted. "I learned a longer one."

"You?" Mavis said. "Well, who am I kidding? I did too."

I could see Lena nodding her head.

I was surprised. I thought it had just been me. "I did too," I said. "I couldn't help myself. Sometimes it just takes you over. I had to read more."

"It calms me down," Jen said. "I know it's hard to believe, but it does. When Mr. Hobbs first told me I reminded him of a guy, I was pretty upset. But after we talked, it made sense. You know what he told me? He said Vachel Lindsay was a guy who acted out his poetry and gave big dramatic readings. A lot of bluster, kind of like me. But then Mr. Hobbs said he'd always thought that on the inside, Lindsay was quieter, more insecure than he let on. I thought that was cool."

"I was reading Edna St. Vincent Millay," Freddie said. "And I realized that all my life I've been looking for a way to show how I feel about things. And then there it was, right on the page. The poetry started making sense to me, as if I could find the answers to people's problems in it."

"That might be going a little overboard," Jen said.

"No, really. It worked. I found one for Brenda."

"For me?" I said.

"Well, what is it?" Jen asked.

"Maybe now's not the right time," Freddie said.

I saw them all looking at me. Even the freshmen kind of scooted over. "It's okay," I said.

Freddie cleared her throat:

*"Childhood is not from birth to a certain age and at a certain age*
*The child is grown, and puts away childish things.*
*Childhood is the kingdom where nobody dies."*

She stopped, and I could feel the girls trying to decide if it was all right to mention death around me. But I wanted to hear it. "Keep going," I whispered.

And she did. She recited the next stanzas about distant relatives, about cats, about how childhood is a kingdom where nobody who matters dies. Then she said:

*"To be grown up is to sit at the table with people who have died,*
*who neither listen nor speak;*
*Who do not drink their tea, though they always said*
*Tea was such a comfort."*

When she finished, I heard only the crackle of the fire. I see my dead brother, I thought. Does that mean I'm grown up now? Then Jen spoke:

*"Let not young souls be smothered out before*
*They do quaint deeds and fully flaunt their pride.*

*It is the world's one crime its babes grow dull,*
*Its poor are ox-like, limp and leaden-eyed.*

*"Not that they starve, but starve so dreamlessly;*
*Not that they sow, but that they seldom reap;*
*Not that they serve, but have no gods to serve;*
*Not that they die, but that they die like sheep."*

"Geez," Lena said. "That is so impressive." I didn't know if she meant the poem or Jen's recitation.

And then Mavis:

*"My feet tug at the floor*
*And my head sways to my shoulder*
*Sometimes when I watch trees sway,*
*From the window or the door.*
*I shall set forth for somewhere,*
*I shall make the reckless choice*
*Some day when they are in voice*
*And tossing so as to scare*
*The white clouds over them on.*
*I shall have less to say,*
*But I shall be gone."*

"I don't know what this all means," I said. "I've learned other poems by Emily Dickinson, but I haven't thought to tell them to anyone."

"I don't think that matters," Jen said. "It's okay."

"No," I said. "No, it does matter. Every little thing matters. That's what I've learned from Emily Dickinson. There's so

191

much detail in life, and I need to pay more attention to it than I have. I want to pay more attention and learn everything I can."

Mavis started crying, and Freddie leaned over to put an arm around her. "What's going on?" she asked.

Mavis tried to talk, but it came out in a whisper. "This is so great," she said. "I don't want it to end. None of it. I want it to go on forever."

"Nothing goes on forever," Jen said.

"But why not?" Mavis wailed. "Why can't it just go on and on?"

"You want to be a kid forever, Mave?" Jen asked. "You can't. We've all got things to do with our lives."

I threw another branch on the fire. "I don't think we should be fighting now," I said.

"Nobody's fighting," said Jen.

"I don't know what to do," Mavis said when the tears had stopped. "With my life, I mean."

Jen grinned. "I know what you can do in the near future. You can steal the ball about seven times a game and do that passing thing you do so well."

Mavis smiled nervously. "And then what?"

"And then you do whatever comes next," Jen said, glancing at me.

The fire was dying, and Mavis rubbed her arms. "But don't you think it's a bad sign?"

"What?"

"That they cut down the tree. Isn't it an omen? Doesn't it mean something bad's going to happen?"

"I hate that their tree's the tallest now," Freddie said.

"We could go over and cut theirs," Jen said. "We did it before; we can do it again."

"No," I said, louder than I meant to.

"No?" said Jen.

"No. What happens when they're both just stumps? What have we proved? That we can kill trees?"

"Oh, boy," Jen said. "I knew you were hanging around Darwin too much."

"Whatever," I said. "It doesn't change the fact that this is our last year. This is our last shot at high school ball. We can't go around thinning out trees until there are none left. That would make us the same as Fostoria. We have to think about tomorrow, and the next day, and next year."

"But do we have to leave?" Mavis asked.

"Hemlock?" I said.

"Yes. I never want to leave here."

"Then stay," Jen said. "Lots of people will be here. Darwin Ostrander will still be here. He's driving to community college every day, but every day he comes back. It'll be like that, Mave. It's okay."

I watched Jen while she talked. She seemed so grown-up then. She knew just what to say.

"Even Brenda's dad'll get a job out of town. And he'll come back, won't he, Brenda?"

Mavis turned and looked at me, and I knew what she wanted me to say.

"You think the best damn basketball player in Hemlock would ever leave Hemlock?" I asked.

"Your dad won't," Jen said. "But you will."

"Yes," I agreed. It must have been how Eric felt when he

told me he was leaving the night we tossed gravel on the street. "I'm leaving town," I whispered.

Tammy stood up and said:

> "I think that I shall never see
> A poem lovely as a tree."

"Uppity freshman," Jen muttered.

But that didn't stop Tammy. When she was through, she started over again, and the rest of us got up too. With our arms over one another's shoulders, we recited together, in unison, as if we'd been doing it all our lives.

> "A tree whose hungry mouth is prest
> Against the sweet earth's flowing breast;
>
> "A tree that looks at God all day,
> And lifts her leafy arms to pray;
>
> "A tree that may in summer wear
> A nest of robins in her hair;
>
> "Upon whose bosom snow has lain;
> Who intimately lives with rain.
>
> "Poems are made by fools like me,
> But only God can make a tree."

There were no big saws grinding or logs splashing or planers whining to drown us out. With nothing to compete with, our words just floated above us and were carried away on the wind.

Over and over again we recited that simple little poem, until we got tired and goofy. I'm sure it was a strange sight: a small high school basketball team, our arms locked together, dancing in a circle around a fire in the middle of winter. But none of us cared how we looked. We all felt like Mavis did: None of us wanted it to end.

# Chapter 22

We left first thing Monday morning. A whole caravan of folks from Hemlock was following our bus. The line of cars snaked back as far as I could see. I picked out Darwin Ostrander's beat-up Chevy, Dante Birmingham's Toyota, Lena's mom and dad in their SUV, and if I squinted my eyes, I could see Eric's Honda beyond that. We made like covered wagons as we labored up and over White Pass in the Cascade Mountains and across the drier parts of the state. Once in a while I'd look out the back window and see my mother driving right behind us. I was sure she'd fought with someone to get that position. She waved at me and put on a good face, but I knew she was worried about our family. Dad hadn't come for the sendoff that morning. Part of me was hoping he was bringing up the rear of the caravan, but I didn't see him the whole trip.

We pulled into Spokane midafternoon and got ourselves

settled into our rooms. The rumor about the bellhops turned out to be true. Jen and I were sharing a room, and we tested our room service about three times before Mr. Hobbs had us get into the bus to go to the practice gym.

Spokane Community College was letting us use their gym, and we shot around, just to keep ourselves loose and focused. A few fans watched us practice, and one of them was Eric. I waved at him and he smiled big. It felt good to have him there.

After a while Mr. Hobbs collected us under one of the baskets and talked about our competition. He said nobody from the west side had won State in about twelve years. He said it was because the girls from the wheat towns and the private schools played very competitive ball.

"They play a different brand of basketball over here," he warned us.

"We can take them," Jen said.

"They don't like to lose," Mr. Hobbs added.

"We're not going to lose," I told him.

And we were right, at least for our first game. We won by twenty-one points, beating a team from the Olympic Peninsula, on our side of the state. The seats were packed with Hemlock fans, and most of them weren't even from Hemlock. A lot of them were from Spokane, because the Spokane paper had done an article on the tournament, featuring our team on the front page. So a lot of these fans were locals, getting their first look at those oddball Lumberjills.

TV cameras were camped all over the place, and someone had hung a sign way up by the sky booths that said RHYME IT!

It all made me a little nervous at first, but after a while I got into it and appreciated having the crowd. I scored twenty-seven points; five of those were free throws that I tossed in without thinking. Luckily the stands in this gym weren't so close to the court, so none of us was shy about reciting. At first the coach on the opposing team laughed when we did it, but he wasn't laughing by the end of the first half.

That night we were on the news, and I saw myself on TV for the first time. I thought I looked skinny and awkward. But Jen said I was smooth, just like Benny.

One game down and three to go to claim the championship. Our next game was scheduled for late afternoon the next day. The more you win, the better game times you get. I could tell all the girls were feeling closer, because we sat right next to one another as we watched the other games. Mr. Hobbs was right about the teams from the east. They played like boys, almost. If someone was in their way, they just bowled her over.

Jen leaned over to me. "Still think we can take them?" she asked.

"Easy," I said.

I still hadn't seen my dad, and at this point I figured he wasn't coming at all. Mom had tried calling around town to find him, but the truth was hardly anyone was left in Hemlock. If your team goes to State, so do you. Even Mrs. Madison, who breathes through a tube and can get around only in a wheelchair, was in Spokane.

The next day we won our second game. And it was against one of those eastern teams. They handled the ball as well as any team I'd ever seen, but our style of play really threw them.

They complained about the poetry, but the ref wouldn't hear it. Pretty soon their coach started hollering at them to quit paying attention, and it was then I knew we had the game won. I scored twenty-one points and pulled down nine rebounds. Winning that game meant we were going to get a trophy. As we walked off the floor, we got a standing ovation from our fans.

I dressed quietly while the girls around me whooped and yelled and pretty much made fools of themselves. Lena read a note she'd gotten from a boy in the stands. She had never been much for dates, but she carefully folded the note and stuck it in her shoe.

When I met my mom outside, I must have looked shaky, because she said right away, "Maybe we'd better get you something to eat."

We went to one of those all-you-can-eat buffets, but I could only get down a salad and a piece of bread. Jen ate most of the chicken wings, and the parents filled their plates to overflowing as they relived the high points of the game.

When we got back to the hotel, one of the cute bellhops held the door open for me. "I saw you on TV," he said as I walked by. "You're good." But I still wasn't feeling quite right, and even that compliment didn't make me feel any better.

Jen and I went up to the room. We sat in the window and tried to pick out who was walking down below. But soon I got restless and went into the bathroom and sat on the edge of the tub. After about fifteen minutes Jen started pounding on the door, asking if I was sick.

I was so on edge, I was worried it was going to happen all over again. That I was going to faint on the floor, and all those thousands of people were going to see how screwed up I really was. I rubbed my palms on my legs.

"I might not be able to do this," I yelled to Jen.

"You have to," she answered.

And she was right. But how?

I tossed and turned all night. I couldn't eat. I couldn't sleep. Finally, I got out of bed and walked down to the lobby. I hung around reading a magazine until I got tired and then went back up to the room. But everything I tried worked for only a little while. Pretty soon I was a nervous wreck again. I think Jen was ready to throw me out. In the morning my eyes were red rimmed and felt as if they had sand in them.

The pressure: I was feeling it everywhere. That night we were playing the defending champions, a team that had been there many times before. Compared with them we were just babes in the woods.

We practiced at the community college again in the afternoon. When I ran into Freddie on a play I knew by heart, it felt like we were back at one of our first practices. Mr. Hobbs's radar went up.

"Miss Dickinson? Is everything all right?"

"Yes," I said angrily.

His eyes got big and he left me alone.

When we practiced free throws, I found out why I was feeling so weird. I recited my lines and had just tossed up the ball when I saw something out of the corner of my eye. I turned and looked. Sitting on a chair under the opposite basket was Benny. Why was this happening again?

It actually made me angry to see him there. "I need a break," I said, and handed the ball over to Mavis. I walked across the court, but as I got closer, I realized this guy looked nothing like Benny. He was a janitor, waiting for us to get done so he could sweep the floor. Mr. Hobbs came up behind me.

"Emily?"

"I don't like my poem," I told him. "I don't like it."

"All right," he said.

"It's about death. It's about waiting for death."

He nodded. "I said all right, Miss Dickinson."

"You mean, I don't have to do it?"

"I didn't say that."

"Well, what, then?"

"I think I'll just leave that up to you."

He walked away, and I turned to see all the girls lined up by the basket. I hated the way they were looking at me. I knew they were wondering if I was going to pass out or say something weird. I took matters into my own hands.

"I am not going crazy," I said flatly.

At the game that night I didn't go out on the court right away. I stood in the corridor and watched the girls on the other team. I was jealous of them. They had beautiful uniforms—a red, white, and blue combination—and a coach who called them by their real names. And I was absolutely sure that none of them had anywhere near the problems I had going on.

Things weren't looking as good down at our end. I hadn't noticed before how skinny Freddie's legs were. And instead of her usual tough-girl look, Jen was daintily picking at her hair, her lips, and her uniform. I was worried.

The first quarter was a disaster. The place was so noisy, I could barely hear Mr. Hobbs from the bench. And the other team was as smooth as mercury rolling across glass. They couldn't miss. Drives to the basket, quick ten-foot jumpers, even three-pointers from way beyond the arc seemed to go through without their even trying. With about three minutes left in the first quarter, Mr. Hobbs called a timeout. We were down, 17–4.

"Miss Dickinson," he said, "this is not the time to be timid. Stand your ground when they come for the attack, and when you want your basket, run them down if you must."

We did better when we came back out, and by the end of the first quarter they were ahead by only eight points, 21–13. Then they took off again in the second quarter. We made a respectable showing and brought the game within three at 36–33, but we got bogged down again. I think we weren't feeling our poets. We may not have been feeling much of anything. The crowd had quieted down so they could hear us recite, but we didn't have our usual kick. Our free-throw percentage was dismal, and Mr. Hobbs was hopping mad.

He tried everything he knew to get us motivated, but nothing was working. And that didn't change until right before the end of the third quarter, when I got fouled. I hadn't been to the line yet, and I dreaded it. I walked up and bounced the ball. But instead of aiming and reciting my poem, I just kept bouncing it.

Bouncebouncebouncebouncebouncebouncebounce.

I couldn't stop because I had started seeing those specks again. The buzz of the crowd echoed around me, like the sound of the ocean in a seashell. I could hear myself saying softly, "Oh, God. Not now. Please." I felt as if I would fall to the floor if I stopped bouncing the ball.

Then I heard myself say, "No more." Not very loud. Just loud enough for me to hear.

It gave me courage, and it quieted my vibrating nerves. I glanced over to Jen, who had a big grin on her face. I looked around at the rest of the team, and they lifted me up to where I needed to be. Free and clear from a lot of things, not just basketball.

Then I did something even I didn't know I was going to do. I chose a different poem. Still Emily Dickinson. But more for me.

I literally shouted it out:

*"It's all I have to bring to-day . . ."*

Bounce-bounce.

*"This, and my heart beside,*
*This, and my heart, and all the fields,*
*And all the meadows wide."*

I aimed at the basket and the ball floated out of my hands. It was as if those words carried it up and through the net.

When I trotted back on defense, I saw Mr. Hobbs standing with his hands on his hips. He seemed to be in a state of wonder. Just like I was. When that happens to you on a basketball court, it sets you free. Nothing matters anymore. Not traveling with the ball. Not having it stolen from you. Not missing the easy lay-up. So you relax. I blocked the next shot by the other team, stole the ball, and ran down the court. As I scored, I was fouled and found myself on the line again. And suddenly, it was as if I remembered every Dickinson poem I'd ever read.

*"I think the hemlock likes to stand . . ."*

Bounce-bounce.

*"Upon a marge of snow . . ."*

Bounce-bounce.

*"It suits his own austerity,*
*And satisfies an awe."*

If I told you how many Dickinson poems I recited in the fourth quarter, you'd know we won the game. The defending champs had lost their touch, but I had found mine.

On my last visit to the charity stripe, I said:

*"I lost a world the other day."*

Bounce-bounce.

*"Has anybody found?"*

Bounce-bounce.

*"You'll know it by the row of stars*
*Around its forehead bound."*

I scored thirty-seven points that game. We won by two. We were going to the finals.

# Chapter 23

I woke up early the next morning. Jen was snoring like a logger, and once I was awake, there was no way I could get back to sleep with that racket. It didn't matter anyway. I needed some time alone and some fresh air. It wasn't hard sneaking out of the hotel, and one of the cute bellhops told me where to go. He even offered to drive me around, but I felt like a walk.

I was invigorated, still buzzing from the night before. Our fans had gone wild when the game ended. It was more than they'd ever hoped for and better than they'd ever known. Better than 1981.

The hotel was right next to a big park in downtown Spokane. I found one of the bridges across the river and walked along the paths. Only a few joggers were out at that hour, so it was nice and quiet.

I was thinking about a year ago and how different everything was then. How I never thought I would make it through.

Sometimes you can't stop crying and you think you're going to shrivel up like a prune because all your tears are leaving. But you don't, and eventually the tears do stop. I'd like to think it's magic, but it takes more work than that.

The Spokane River is cut in half by an island. Half the river is dammed up, and the other side drops down in a waterfall. I walked over to the side where the water was roaring over the rocks.

There's a suspension footbridge across the falls, wide enough for two people. The spray was misting over it, making the surface foggy and slick, and I walked out to the middle to think.

The mill was never going to reopen. Everyone in town was grasping that. If you read the paper or looked at the news at night, you could see that the lumber business wasn't what it used to be. People couldn't afford wood the way they used to, and the sad news was that there wasn't much of it left anymore. The world of Hemlock was changing. Some houses might go up for sale. A few stores might close. But some would open up again, like Marv's Videos. Or better yet, My Mom's Videos. And maybe new ones would open too. Businesses that the new Hemlock would need. The town wouldn't dry up completely. In spite of the bad in life, there's always got to be hope.

I was thinking about all that when I saw Benny step onto the footbridge from the other side. I checked my pulse. Unlike all the times before, this time it was normal. My palms weren't sweaty. I wasn't mad about anything. In fact, this time it was as if I held the strings and he was moving his arms and legs at my command.

As he walked forward, it was like the mist blew right

through him. But he still looked good, like he used to when he walked in front of the mirror and swished a comb through his hair like Elvis did in the old movies. Immediately, as if he knew what I was thinking, he took out a comb and ran it through his hair. I laughed out loud. Even above the roar of the falls, I could hear him and he could hear me.

"Hello, Benny," I said.

"Hello, Sis."

"I'm trying to think what I should tell you about."

"Take your time," he said. "That's something I've got plenty of."

"But I don't," I said.

"Sure you do."

I shook my head. "I don't think so, Benny. I've got to move on."

"I was wondering about that. Any way I can convince you to stay?"

"You were a great player and a great brother, Benny. That will never change."

"I guess that makes me immortal."

My teeth chattered, and I wrapped my arms around me. "Well, we made it to the finals."

"I know. Congratulations." He smiled sadly.

And then it hit me in the gut. "And here you are, Benny. Guess you made it to State too."

"Thanks to you. You've got pretty broad shoulders, Sis."

"I'm sorry," I said. "I'm sorry I changed the poem at the line last night. I just couldn't do it anymore. Do you understand that? I couldn't keep saying it, couldn't keep talking and thinking about death."

He nodded. "It had to happen sooner or later. I'm surprised you could memorize all those other poems."

"I'm kind of tired of it. Tired of being Emily Dickinson and waiting for the next bad thing to happen."

"I get it, Brenda," he said. He put his hand out. "I have to tell you one more thing."

"What is it?"

"I want to tell you I'm sorry for dying on you. I was just feeling so good that night—"

"You don't have to say that," I interrupted. "I know it already." But hearing those words come from him made me wonder about what Darwin had told me. Was everything Benny said coming from inside me? I decided to test it out. "Benny, are we going to win tonight?"

For a moment it was like the sun had risen between us and lit up our faces. We smiled, both knowing he didn't have the answer to that question.

"I can't tell the future, Brenda."

I nodded and knew then I would never see my brother again. It was bittersweet. I let my sadness linger a moment longer and then felt it rise up and into the fog. I was tired of fighting. Tired of raging against the dying of the light.

We were quiet for a while. Or I was quiet for a while. Only the river roared below us. Like I said, silence has a voice, and I knew what it was saying now.

"I've got to get going," I finally said.

"I know."

But I was suddenly desperate to remember everything I'd forgotten to tell him. "Benny, you heard about the tallest tree in Lewis County? Mavis's parents moved to Olympia. Mom and Dad are separated. I lead the tournament in scoring—"

"Brenda," he said, interrupting me, "you already know these things."

"That's right," I said. "I do."

We stood opposite each other for a moment, and then he turned and walked back into the fog. I didn't feel the need to run after him, to shout out his name, to ask him to stay with me the rest of my life. I just stood there and felt a little homesick, a little sad. The kind of feeling I could live with.

Later, when we went to the arena to watch the consolation games, I saw a reporter filming people. When I got closer, I realized he was shooting them reciting poetry. Mrs. Hobbs was there, saying:

*"Once upon a midnight dreary, while I pondered, weak and weary . . ."*

One by one, fans were stepping up to the mike and telling the world their favorite poems. Even Jen's little brother got all giggly and said:

*"I never saw a Purple Cow;*
*I never hope to See One;*
*But I can Tell you, Anyhow,*
*I'd rather See than Be One."*

Everybody in Hemlock, and Spokane too, had a screw loose. Maybe everyone in the whole world. Mr. Hobbs was a wise man after all. All these people I'd never thought would have gotten together to even look at poetry were here fighting for the opportunity to recite it.

"Change is good," I said. But I was the only one who heard me.

During halftime of the second game I saw Ms. Cochran looking up into the stands. I stood and waved at her, and she pointed a finger. Next to her was another woman, and the two of them walked up the steps to see me.

"I can't believe how well you all are playing," Ms. Cochran said, giving me a hug. "And you, Brenda, you look like the WNBA out there."

I shrugged and felt foolish.

"This is Louise Brown," Ms. Cochran said. "You know, the coach at the University of Oregon?"

The woman had a powerful grip and a great wide smile. "We've spoken on the phone," she said.

"I remember," I told her.

"I've been watching you, young lady," she said. "I must say, after watching the game films Mr. Hobbs sent me and from what I've seen so far in this tournament, I'm very pleased to see that you applied to our school. More than pleased." She nodded her head toward Ms. Cochran. "And I can't seem to get your old coach out of my hair. She keeps saying to me, 'Have you come to a decision about Brenda Jacobsen?'"

"I don't know what to say," I said.

"Say you'll meet with me before you go back home," she said.

"I'll meet with you before I go back home," I agreed.

"Now, that wasn't so hard, was it?"

"I guess not," I said.

"But I think we may have a problem, young lady."

"Oh, no," I said. "What?"

"I'm afraid we don't do poetry on the foul line."

I laughed. "I think I can live with that."

We talked a few more minutes until the game started up again. Ms. Brown gave me her card, and I looked at it long after they walked back to their seats. When I finally looked up, I saw Eric sitting across the aisle. Not a vision, but a real person.

There was still no sign of my dad when we got to the arena at five thirty that evening. Part of me wondered if I would ever see him again, but I tried to put that thought out of my mind. I had more important things to think about.

In the finals we were playing a team like us. They didn't recite poetry, but just like us they weren't expected to be in the finals. Mr. Hobbs said that made them more dangerous, because they were as hungry as we were. I didn't know about that. I didn't think anyone was as hungry as we were.

It was a full house, which meant a crowd in the thousands. It was also being televised by the local station. By the time we went out to do our warm-ups, the place was packed. The pep bands were wailing, one song after another, and TV cameras were dragging long cables back and forth across the court. I almost tripped over one, and Mr. Hobbs was out like a shot, telling them to "remove those foul bearers of bad news."

My mom sat in a folding chair at one end of the court. She had her bags of snacks and was staring down the usher, who was giving her the evil eye.

Before the game we were all introduced in front of the television cameras. Jen said, "Hi, Mom," real loud and got a big cheer from the fans. When the whistle blew, I won the tip-off and we scored the first basket of the game.

It took a few minutes, but then I got into it. Like I had at the end of the game before, I was playing somewhere deep in my unconscious. The ball floated from my hands and through the hoop. Freddie was on fire too. She dribbled like she was trying to stamp out an anthill on the hardwood. We were all having our best game. By the end of the first quarter we were leading, 14–7. If we held on, in twenty-four minutes we would be the new state champions.

The idea made goose bumps break out on my arms and forced me to bear down even harder in the second quarter. We were a perfectly synchronized machine on a mission. The beauty of the game played out in the way our team moved. It was just as Mr. Hobbs had predicted: The poets were our alter egos, and the rhythm flowed through our souls. We could have closed our eyes and still found our way to the basket. I did that once, as a matter of fact. I drove toward the lane and closed my eyes. The ball went up and through the hoop. And when I turned and opened my eyes, I saw my dad standing on the sidelines.

As I moved closer to him, I could see he was all cleaned up. But at first I couldn't read the look on his face. I had visions of him stomping out on the court and ruining the game. But as I passed, a glorious smile broke out on his face. "Get 'em, Brenda!" he called as I ran down on defense.

To hear that coming from my dad, the very words he had used to urge Benny on, lifted me higher than I had ever felt on a basketball court. I couldn't contain my excitement. My nerves, my muscles, everything was electrified. I clapped my hands and shouted to the team, "Let's get 'em!"

The last two minutes of the half took no time as we dominated the game. By the time the buzzer sounded, I was walking a few inches above the ground. As I strode off the court, though, I saw my dad take off for one of the exits, and I hit the earth with a thud.

"No," I groaned. I ran over and found Mr. Hobbs. "I'll be there in a sec," I said.

He looked skeptical, but I didn't give him time to complain. I slipped on my sweats, then headed out the exit to the parking lot. It was dark and cold out, but the night sky was full of stars. I found both my parents sitting on one of the big boulders in front of the building.

Seeing the two of them together like that, I thought they might as well have been a couple of kids doing detention. I expected the worst.

"Is everything okay?" I asked.

Dad nodded. "I just needed some air. It's been a long time, you know."

"I was worried when I saw you leave. And I can't be worried right now. I've got a game to play in there."

"I know," he said. "You don't have to worry."

Not sure, I turned to my mother. "Mom?"

She patted my dad on the arm. "It's going to be okay, Brenda."

I needed to go, but I couldn't leave them until I said one more thing. "When we get back home, the first thing I want to do is go down to the shop. I want you, Dad, and whoever else you can find to put me up against the doorjamb and measure me. I want you to make a mark there with my name and the date on it. Then I want you to do it for each and every one of the girls on the team. No matter what happens tonight, I want you to do that."

"All right," Dad said. "I'll make it happen."

I leaned in and hugged them both. "And I want us all to sit down and figure out how we're going to do this from now on. Understood?"

"Understood," they said in unison.

I left my parents there in front of the arena. Later, I would come to realize that I left them in more ways than one. It's what happens. If you're human, sooner or later you'll want to leave. I see it as a little like poetry. Sometimes you have to look at all the stanzas of your life and realize it's time to change your poem. You might even have to check out other poets. But what do I know? My personal life's poem is just beginning.

I opened the door to the arena and felt the warm air rush out to greet me. I had a strange feeling that this was a good omen. Like Benny's breath carrying me forward. I liked the idea, and I trotted back across the hall to the team. Win or lose, I think I was finally ready for the second half.